KT-422-272

Danda

Nkem Nwankwo

Fontana / Collins

First published by André Deutsch Ltd 1964
First issued on Fontana Books 1972
Second Impression March 1973
Third Impression January 1975
Fourth Impression September 1977
Fifth Impression May 1980

© Nkem Nwankwo 1964

Made and printed in Great Britain
William Collins Sons and Co Ltd Glasgow

CONDITIONS OF SALE
This book is sold subject to the condition
that it shall not, by way of trade or otherwise, be lent, re-sold, hired out or otherwise
circulated without the publisher's prior
consent in any form of binding or cover
other than that in which it is published and
without a similar condition including this
condition being imposed on the subsequent
purchaser

A·99 R.J.Drakeford

Danda

'Let me ask you, does day reach your hut or not? How long do you want to sleep? Are you a white man?'

Danda heard only dimly these questions fired at him with such rapidity. He stirred drowsily, yawned and said 'eh?'

'What is "eh"? Is today a feast day?' Araba sniffed angrily and went back to his obi.

Danda yawned again and slowly slid his right leg down the raised mud which served him as a bed. Then mentally he dared the other leg to follow. This limb declined to. The first leg hesitated, gave in and returned to its partner. Danda sighed cosily and went back to sleep.

Fontana African Novels

The Madness of Didi   *Obi Egbuna*
Elina   *Obi Egbuna*
The Bride Price   *Buchi Emecheta*
Second Class Citizen   *Buchi Emecheta*
The Slave Girl   *Buchi Emecheta*
The Naked Gods   *Chukwuemeka Ike*
The Potter's Wheel   *Chukwuemeka Ike*
The Guardian of the Word   *Camara Laye*
The African Child   *Camara Laye*
A Dream of Africa   *Camara Laye*

CHAPTER ONE

The boat caused a stir throughout Aniocha as it wound its way through snaky pathways, brushed past scorched bushes, swerved from tall palms and then came to rest in the shade of an ogbu tree, in front of a big iron house. The owner climbed out, and as he did so, he gave a sharp order to the driver. Then he turned and waved cheerfully to the many people who had gathered to admire his boat. He was of medium height, stocky, with scarred face and sharp eyes which were not sure whether to twinkle or to be suspicious. His agbada, made from brown prints, seemed to belong to a smaller man so that it hadn't many of its usual superfluous folds. The man walked briskly with an impetuous gait and soon entered into the iron house.

The many people who had followed the progress of the land-boat with awe now came from several directions and surrounded it. They had seen many of its likes before but this was the first to be owned by an Aniocha man.

'Ahai,' said a herdsman, 'it shines like lightning. I wonder how much it costs. Can the money in all Aniocha buy it?'

'Impossible.'

'I look like a spirit,' said an old woman peering dimly at her image distorted on the body of the car.

'Wait, people of my land,' said the herdsman, listening, 'our man!'

Bells were heard tinkling in unison at a distance. The attention of the crowd was at once drawn away from the boat.

'Rain!' they said, turning delighted, expectant faces towards the direction from which it blew.

A little later, a lithe, tall man turned a corner and lunged towards the group. This was Danda, otherwise known as 'Rain'. The tinkles came with him. They were produced by small, bronze bells which were sown on to a blue cloak lined with white which draped him from shoulder to ankle.

'Rain!' many shouted again, and some 'is he drunk?'
'Hoa!' roared the newcomer. His clear-cut features were
very expressive, his eyes laughing 'kliklikli!' he shouted.

'Yiii!' returned the crowd.

.'Kliklikli!'

'Yiii!'

'I give to each man his own. Goodness to all. If there is
any man to whom what is good is not good let him put his
head into the fire and see how he likes it.'

There was much more flourish after this, some wiseacres
chaffing Rain and he riposting aptly. Then he said, pointing
to the land-boat:

'Do they say this is our brother's?'

'It belongs to Ndulue Oji.'

'Man of our family?'

'True word.'

'So this world is ours?'

'Ahai!'

Rain stood thinking for a moment. Then coming to a
decision he walked to the car, opened its back door and
climbed in. 'Ahai,' he sighed trying the cushion, 'world that
is good.'

'That is the way it is done,' said the herdsman, grinning.
'If my bottom were strong, I would do the same.'

The driver of the car had gone somewhere to drink water,
and soon returned. He was dressed in white overalls and
peaked cap.

'What next,' he said as he saw Rain. 'You are brave!'
Rain peeped out of the window. 'Does he say it is what?'
he said.

'Come out,' roared the driver.

'If I were hungered to, I would break his head,' said Rain.

'Do you come out or may I chuck you out!' shouted the
driver, beside himself.

'People of our land,' said Rain, 'but for my bowing to your
eyes I would break this boy's head. He has fired my anger.'

The old woman intervened. 'You can't talk to him that

way, my son,' she said to the driver. 'He is not your age group.'

'And while we are talking, the land-boat does not belong to you,' said another woman. 'I can't understand these boys.'

'Get going, old bones,' said the driver.

The women shrank away. At this moment two men came by, one of them wore the anklets of the ozo. The driver appealed to them.

'There is a rascal dirtying my master's car,' he said. 'What does he look like?' They poked their heads into the car. 'Ah, it is Danda.'

'Come out,' the ozo man said. 'Can't you see you have not grown fit for this type of thing?'

'Men who go about in land-boats have horns?' said Danda, turning to the crowd and inviting them to applaud the quip.

They did.

'Come out,' said the ozo. He disliked Danda's persistence the more so as he would have liked to get into the land-boat if he got the chance. 'If every akalogholi is to ride a land-boat, there will be nothing left for the world to do but turn upside down.'

'Men of our land,' said Danda, still keeping the sympathy of the crowd, 'did you not tell me that this land-boat belongs to one of my brothers?'

'Therefore it is yours!' roared the herdsman delightedly. 'What belongs to one belongs to one's kindred. Ho ha!'

The appearance of the owner of the car put an end to further altercation. Ndulue Oji had just said farewell to his host and came waddling out. He saw the people gathered about his car and was pleased. Some ten years ago he had gazed like them at one of the wonders of the white man. It hadn't occurred to him that he would one day own it. But the war had enriched him, the eyes of his fathers had been open.

'People of our land, I greet you,' he said, with a great laugh, shaking hands with a few. Then he put his hand to the handle of the door of his car but stopped, furious.

'Who is this fellow?' he said glaring at the driver.

'He got in when I went to drink water. And I cannot pull him out.'

Ndulue looked more closely, and recognizing the intruder, smiled. 'Ah it is you, brother,' he said. He liked Danda.

'Is it Ndulue's voice I hear?' asked Danda.

'Yes, come out!'

'Take me home in this our land-boat.'

'No, you can ride in it any other day but today.'

'Now.'

'No, come out,' said Ndulue, raising his voice slightly.

'Well, if I were you I would listen, Danda,' said the herdsman, conciliating Ndulue.

Danda thought for a moment and then said: 'You think you can turn me out of this land-boat?'

'Yes.'

'You are not fit to.'

'Danda is right,' murmured the old woman. 'Does the law say now that when a man has a land-boat he should forget his kindred!'

Ndulue was beaten. He had made his mark in the world and like most Aniocha arrivers he was now cultivating the goodwill of his neighbours. The last thing he wanted was for it to get about that he had refused a member of his kindred hospitality. So, smiling, he nodded to the driver, got in himself, and sat beside Danda.

The crowd clapped their hands.

'Thank you,' said Danda. 'And farewell. Stay on the ground and eat sand. Danda is flying to the land of the spirits on the wings of the eagle.'

The car cruised past the new beautiful church of the Anglican mission, past the small haberdashery that had recently been opened by one of Ndulue's friends and past the huge sign post that directed people to the Roman Catholic mission on the other side of the village.

'It is a fine world,' said Danda.

'True,' agreed Ndulue.

Soon they arrived at the big compound walled round with

iron and drove through the stylish door. The house was two-storied, and was famous all over Aniocha. The plan was after that of a District Officer whom Ndulue had known when he was abroad. This was the man who used to kick him playfully on the shins. But the agonies had won Ndulue the contracts for building prisoners' quarters.

There was a garage at the right and the car was parked in it. The men came out.

'We have done it, son of our fathers,' said Ndulue, watching Danda.

'It was good. We ate the world,' said Danda leading the way into the two-storied house.

'There are people in the shed,' continued Ndulue. Since he completed the house he had become increasingly annoyed with the villagers coming into it, sometimes still carrying their work dirt, sitting firmly on the new cushion chairs and saying challengingly 'this house is as much mine as yours.' To stop them he had built a long shed which faced the main building, and given orders that anybody who wanted palm wine should go there. But a few of the men of whom Danda was one had never recognized the demarcation. 'I have no oji in my parlour,' said Ndulue.

'Never mind,' said Danda.

Two strangers were already in the parlour. Danda greeted them in his usual way.

'Kliklikli.'

'Yii.'

'Welcome, strangers,' said Danda. 'Aniocha is safe for you. The man who comes to visit should not bring in evil, neither should he carry evil away.'

At the sight of his visitors Ndulue was excited. One was a merchant friend of his, a thin man who wore an oversize agbada and an old pair of spectacles. The other was a young senior service man dressed quietly in a black suit.

'Are these your faces?' Ndulue roared. He embraced the trader and shook hands with the young man.

'We came a short while ago,' said the former, 'and they said you had not gone far so we decided to wait.'

'You did well, ha!' He embraced the trader again and laughed loud and long.

After that he bustled about with a strained, preoccupied expression. 'There is no oji in this house,' he said at last. 'This is too bad.' Then he said: 'Very well. Okoli Oka!' A stalwart servant in shorts and singlet burst into the room.

'What!' bawled Ndulue. 'Go and dress well, damn fool!' The steward ran back to the servants' quarters. Some minutes later he came back dressed this time in white overalls and white trousers but no shoes.

'Go and get me the hot drink.'

'We were invited for the feast by our relatives here,' the merchant said after the steward had gone.

'Your relatives?' said Ndulue. 'Have you relatives in Aniocha?'

'Yes, didn't you know? My great grandmother on the father's side was married from here.'

'True word!'

The steward came in carrying a tray with a bottle of brandy and three glasses.

'Martell!' announced Ndulue grabbing the bottle roughly. 'Make friends with Martell!' He uttered this phrase a little self-consciously. It was one of the few English expressions he knew.

The brandy was to be drunk neat. He carefully measured out some potion into the three glasses. Then he took one and waved the other two on to his guests.

There was in the parlour a long massive table which ran the whole length of the room. The visitors sat on one side of it, Danda and Ndulue on the other. Now before the steward could reach the guests he had to pass Danda and walk right round the table.

Danda had been standing, telling the merchant a story. As soon as the steward came abreast of him he took one of the glasses and continued his story.

The steward stared, undecided.

'Why did you bring only three glasses?' shouted Ndulue. 'Have I now become so poor that I have to stint glasses?

Isn't he very stupid?' he said to his visitors.

The merchant laughed.

'Come, take this and serve my own friends. Get another glass for me. And mind, I am tired of your fumbling. I will sack you.'

'Yes, sir.' The steward disappeared again to fetch the fourth glass. Ndulue filled it for himself and then said in English:

'Cheers!'

'Cheers,' responded his guests standing.

'Cheers,' said Danda also standing.

'Long life and prosperity,' said Ndulue again in English. The guests raised their glasses aloft.

At the end of the ritual they were about to sit down but Danda said:

'Wait, people of our land. Let us do this thing as it is done.' They were puzzled but remained standing.

Danda turned to Ndulue and said, 'Let's have one more drink. If we have to have wine we may as well have enough to fill our mouths.'

'True word,' said the trader measuring out some more drops of brandy.

'That's how it is,' said Danda raising his glass. 'When a man brings oji we must pray to his ofo. We thank you, Ndulue. We pray that from where you got this oji there will be more of it for you. A hundred more. Let us pray to Chineke Olisaebuluwa who made all things. Chineke, come down from the sky and eat oji. Spirits of the dead come and eat oji.' Danda tipped some liquid on the floor.

Ndulue had waited with some impatience for the end of the story. At last he said 'Son of our fathers—'

'The world is bad nowadays,' said Danda. 'Let the world be good. Let this oji cleanse the world. Let it make us friends. May each man have what is due to him. The hawk shall perch and the eagle shall perch. Whichever bird says to the other don't perch let its wings break.' And Danda tossed the drink into his mouth and sighed gustily.

The others sat down.

'How is our business?' Ndulue said to the civil servant who till now had said nothing.

'It goes on.'

'Have they seen the face of our paper yet?'

'Not yet.' He was an Assistant District Officer. A month before, his superior had advertised for contractors to build some culverts in a Native Authority road. Ndulue had prepared his tender and had passed it to the young officer asking him to try his best to see it through.

'We shall see what can be done,' said the ADO.

But apparently this reply was not sufficiently reassuring. Ndulue had waited on the young man, pressed him to his house, given him Martell.

'We shall see what can be done.' The ADO stuck to this noncommittal position. The trouble was that though he had often accepted gifts he hadn't learnt how to give them. They said that the safest way was to deal through the District Officer's steward. But even this method spelled its own peril. 'We shall do our best,' he repeated warily.

'It is well,' said Ndulue. 'I don't understand white men. I have never been to England. You have been, and I know you know how to deal with our man. It is good for a man to have legs in many places.'

There was a lull in the conversation after this. And Danda who couldn't bear silence dispelled it. He sang in a husky-sweet voice shaking his head from side to side and occasionally stopping to bawl: 'Ewe ewe ewe! that's the way we do it!'

'Rain,' said Ndulue smiling. And then to the guests as if explaining Danda's aberration: 'He is my brother.'

'Ewe ewe ewe!' Danda continued braying. After some minutes he made an end. Then he carefully untied from a thick knot at the edge of his wrapper a beautifully carved oja and began to flute with it. The silvery sounds darted up to the ceiling ruffling the cobwebs at the four corners of the room and bringing to life the clod-like statues that stood in framed family pictures on the wall.

'Oi! Oi! Oi!' cried Danda, moved to ecstasy by his own

fluting. Then he drew an impudent finale and waited for the type of applause he was used to. There was none. Danda burst.

'Why are we so solemn? Why are we dressed up? Have we forgotten how to stand on our heads?' Danda stood on his head. And waved his legs in the air.

'Why don't we eat pepper?' he said as he regained his feet. 'No, I am not drunk. But why are we dumb. Dance, shout, laugh. Eat pepper. Shake hands!' He shook hands with all of them.

At last the visitors took their leave. Ndulue, fussing insistently, saw them out.

Danda stood on the top of the cement steps in front of the house and watched the golden ridges moulded by the departing sun.

'Rain has been entertained in the house,' whispered an occupant of the shed to a friend.

'He doesn't go for small things, Rain.'

'God created the world,' cried Danda. He cleaned the saliva off the oja and began to flute again calling the praise names of the men who sat in the shed.

One of them leapt out and ran towards the farther wall of the compound shouting 'ewe ewe ewe!' His praise name had been mentioned by the oja and this had made him mad. 'Ewe ewe ewe!' he roared stopping precariously only a pace from the corrugated iron cover of the wall. Then he ran back to his place still bawling.

Ndulue had come back now and was free to work himself up to the same level of excitement as the rest.

'That's how it is, flute man,' he cried as he heard his praise name fluted. 'I hear you!' He ran into his house, and a minute later returned, carrying a double-barrelled gun, loaded it, and let off two volleys into the heavens.

'Sing on. You are in my house and no evil can fall on you. It is I, Ndulue, who say you should sing.' He thumped his chest for emphasis and laughed his mighty laugh.

The last strains of the song trailed away. Then Danda crying 'oi! oi! oi!' sprinted out of the compound.

Nnoli Nwego, a giant of a man with huge shoulders and a small head, detached himself from the other people in the shed and joined him.

'I have eaten the world,' Danda said to him.

'Did Ndulue give you palm wine?'

'I am not drunk.'

'You said you ate the world!'

'I fled to the land of the spirits on the wings of the eagle,' Danda said.

CHAPTER TWO

'We are late,' Nnoli said.

'The day is long yet,' said Danda.

Since the morning the festival had been warming up. Most of the spirits of ancestors had already emerged from ant-holes in the ground, rejoiced with their brothers and sunk back to the home of the dead. The dancing groups had all been to the shrine of Obunagu, the father of the town, and after that separated and gone their various ways to various dancing centres about the town. The roads were deserted. And the only sign of the feast that remained was the children whose mouths were oily oily and who were running round the lanes blowing the crops of slaughtered chicken to make balloons. There was also the spume of chicken down that rose with the harmattan. It had long been the custom to spray the approaches to a householder's compound with the feathers of chicken. The quantity of feathers had come to be an index of a man's standing in the community. The more of it there was the more the number of chickens he could afford to kill and therefore the greater his wealth would be taken to be. So there was no doubt that Danda's family was of first consequence, for as he made his way into the compound he had to step on a thick carpet of feathers. When he returned he carried an ngwu agelega or ozo staff.

'Yours or your father's?' Nnoli asked.

'I have just made it!' Danda had a forge in his hut and often tinkered about there producing at long intervals small hoes and knives.

'The ozos will be at you,' said Nnoli.

'They are not fit.'

'Does one need to tell a deaf man when war has broken out?' They were now treading the old laterite road. Aniocha boasts two main streets. One, tarred, well maintained, skirts the side of the village and leads away to the District Headquarters and beyond. The other divides Aniocha into two, is rutted and uncared for so that in the scorch season, as now, it exudes a cloud of dust. But the two men walked jauntily through the fumes. After some time they came before a small compound squatting amidst a group of bamboos. Danda stopped, cupped his hand to his mouth and made a bird-call. A small girl emerged from the old rutted gate.

'Is Okoli Mbe there?' Danda asked.

'No, he has gone to the ebe.'

'It is well, my daughter,' said Danda.

'We are not in time,' Nnoli said. And then 'oi oi oi! We hear you. We are on our way!' He was answering the call of the ekwe which had been cracking out like a mad dog from a short distance ahead.

'My father bore me well, my chi created me well!' cried Danda, sprinting down an embankment.

The two had now left the main road and were running along a valley created by the rain as it ate its way through soft earth. On both sides were mud palm-thatched huts closely embracing the woods.

The music rose higher, the ogene was now to be heard in all its mellifluousness insinuating into the blood. The two men breathed hard.

'My father bore me well—' Danda called out. He put his flute to his mouth and sent a short reply over the trees to the musicians. Some children watched the performance wedged between the bamboos at the sides of the trench.

'Sons and daughters!' Danda laughed. To the boys he

said: 'When your father quarrels with your mother take the part of the father for he owns the home.' And to the girls: 'Don't worry your heads over husbands; I will find them for you.'

A little further down the path they came face to face with a plumpish young woman who at once broke out into a merry ripple. This was Ekeama Idemmili the wife of the chieftain's son.

'My wife,' Danda said.

'My husband,' said Ekeama, closing, crinkling her eyes, archly shaking her large ear-rings.

Danda stretched his hand and smacked her bottom.

'Oh—' she frowned but the next moment bubbled over. Coyly she looked down on herself, at her breasts and her multi-coloured wrapper, then satisfied, crinkled her eyes again breaking out into her loud 'hahaha!'

'Bad woman. When do I come for that bitter-leaf soup?'

'Bad man . . . After you have worked for it.' She walked on, but after a few paces spoke over her shoulder 'Sometime.'

'Great woman,' said Danda and set off again followed by Nnoli Nwego.

A fence had been erected across the path by a man who claimed that the valley was part of his land and should not be a highway. The two men did what everybody would do, jumped the fence. Then they cleared the embankment and were before the king of the spirits himself.

The drummers, dwarfed to the size of ants, had surrounded him and been trying to make him hear them. The king heard them and nodded at the homage. And the multi-coloured plume on his polished crown brushed the skies.

The Ijele is the pride of Aniocha. People from all lands come to us either to buy palm wine or to see the Ijele. And because of this the Iklolo family who by tradition raise the king feel that if nothing else, this entitles them to a position of first consequence.

For five days before the festival their women had

walked round Aniocha pleading with the king to leave his
realm underground and come to the land of men.

> 'It is us big masquerade
> We are looking for Ijele
> The King of masquerades.'

At last, just as the sun was reaching the middle of the sky
this day the king of the spirits emerged. And the earth
trembled at each step he took.

As ornaments he carried with him complete worlds. The
first which belted him round the waist was the human
world of beautiful men and women, lions, birds, which did
not look so much carved out of wood as real. Then there
was the world of dead heroes, warriors, men who rode on
horses, carried bows and arrows, hunted the stick-legged
deer. The enormous chest was circled by a world of
mirrors which flashed blindingly as the king swayed to the
rhythm of the drums.

Danda joined the musicians, turned up his oja and found
his place in the rhythm. The chirrup of the flute wound in
and out of the other instruments informing them with
exquisite melody.

The Ijele listened and swayed and nodded with pleasure.
Then he began to dance. There was great excitement. People
surged nearer but were beaten back by young men placed
in good positions for the purpose.

The Ijele danced. And at every step he took, at the
impact of his ponderous feet on the ground, the earth
groaned: 'Jim . . . jim!' It was like the sound a giant pestle
would make on a giant mortar. The pressure of the crowd
against the barrier was mounting and the young men were
finding it difficult to hold their positions. But soon the
drums began to fade and that was a signal for the Ijele to
retire. The king began his return journey brushing the sky
with his multi-coloured plume. The distance was not far but
the Ijele walked slowly as befitted the head of the masquerades. The crowd had broken through the cordon and

were milling round the departing deity. But he reached his fence safely and sank down an ant-hole to the world of the dead.

Women dancers then came into the dancing circle to celebrate the triumph of the Ikolo umunna.

Danda sought a more exciting scene.

'The Apiti umunna are bringing out the Agbogho Mmonwu,' said Nnoli Nwego.

'True word,' said Danda and began to flute.

The Apitis are the smallest family group in Aniocha, and in fact for long they had been urged to merge with some of the larger families. But they had stuck to their independence. They had their own ebe and on feast days clustered about it and heard their own drummers and watched their own masquerade. This last was a girl spirit ushered in by gaily-dressed drummers. Their music was tender and ritualistic. The Agbogho Mmonwu did not dance but merely walked the ebe spraying the crowd with maize ears for fertility. She sprayed Danda, too, as he joined her followers and praised her with the flute—

The day, as Danda would say, was almost complete. Danda had been to most ebes in the village, he had made himself conspicuous in the Umunze family, he had engaged in a fight with masqueraders of the Uruezu umunna, he had preached to a crowd at the Uruoji gathering: 'If there is a man to whom what is good is not good let him dig his own grave and see how he likes it.' Then, followed by Nnoli, he came home to the Uwadiegwu umunna to which he belonged. They were only just in time to see the izaga—stilt-spirit.

The izaga held on to a bamboo post, fanning himself with a feather fan. That fan contained a powerful ogwu without which the izaga would be blown off his spindle legs and come crashing to the earth.

The spectators waited breathlessly. Some rich people threw pennies up to the izaga. He caught them and dropped them into the pockets of his enormous skirt but his old, leathery face, framed by a white goatish beard, showed little gratitude or animation. He was afraid. The izaga dance

18

is a perilous one, perilous for the dancer. For there are always among the spectators some malevolent dibias who would want to try out the power of a new ogwu by pulling the izaga down. To counter the nsi the izaga needed to be as strong as dried wood. And even then he can still be made to succumb. Only last week an Eziakpaka izaga who was well known for being strong in ogwu had crashed and filled his kindred with shame. The Uwadiegwu spirit was taking no chances.

'Get out!' he shrieked. 'Get out!' he waved his fan nervously. The spectators turned on the object of the izaga's fury, an old, dried-up man whose head shone bright and sinister. Nwibe Nwalusi's fame as a magician, dibia, and evil genius had spread all over the world.

'Get back home. This is no place for you—'

The people began to mutter angrily. Nwibe Nwalusi was not an Uwadiegwo but had strayed in from the Ikolo umunna.

'You cannot harm me!' cried the izaga becoming a little hysterical. 'I have never offended you. The whole of Aniocha will stand behind me. You cannot take sand from my footprints—'

Voices of protest swelled from all sides. Many railed at the magician, some young men actually advanced menacingly to within a few feet of the demon. But that was as far as they could go for his medicine froze them.

'Why do you want to ruin me. I have never crossed your path—' Through all this hubbub the demon had sat unconcerned, slyly caressing a deadly fetish that lay across his knees, reeking of ogwu. At last, calmly, taking his time, he got up and crept away, ignoring the taunts of the world.

The drums shook off restraint, woke, and thundered. The izaga danced, flinging his needle legs about precariously, shaking like a tall bamboo caught in the wind. There were wild cheers. But experts in such things said the izaga was only second rate; he was nothing for instance to the izaga of Eziakpaka. However, throughout his performance all but the most hard-boiled had carried their hearts in their mouths. And for a majority who made no claim to be experts in the izaga dance this was what mattered.

The ebe overflowed. Men had crept in from the surrounding umunnas and there was jostling for a better view. Young boys climbed the numerous ogbu trees. And there they stuck like bees, buzzing. One member of the cluster, a plump urchin, peeled away and broke his fall on the head of a thin rake of a herdsman. The victim, winded, squatted on the dust for a long time gasping. Then, recovering, he lit out after the culprit.

The ceremony was now approaching its climax. A new dance group had come into the ebe, making its way through the exhilarated crowd to the dancing circle. Danda led them with his flute. Nnoli had cut a stick from the bush nearby and with it was beating the ground, clearing the people and making way for the dancers.

'Hai! Hai! Take your heavy bodies off!' he shouted. The nervous crowd, cursing him heartily, collapsed against one another, shrieking. The drummers took a position below an ogbu tree and began to perform.

You have probably heard that music: the nervous agony of the ekwe, the poignant melancholy of the oja, the clamorous swell of the drums and the plaintiveness of the ogene; all combining to bring down the sky with lusty pulsation, to create the rhythm that some say was brought back from the land of the spirits by the great Ojadili: he who wrestled with the ten-headed king of the spirits and made the monarch's back kiss mother earth; the music that for ages has led Aniocha men to rage in riotous abandon, that takes a small drop of the day and inflates it into a tempestuous sea in which the men and women drowned, that snatches from time one small moment and gives it the vastness of eternity.

'Cle-tum cle-tum cle-tum!' And the world was annihilated. Our dance too is like our music, obstreperous; it does not suggest or insinuate it states boldly, crudely. And what it has to say is very much after our hearts. It made Dand, mad. Running wildly to a section of the crowd he greeted them:

'Kliklikli!'

'Yiii!'

'Kliklikli—'

'Yiii—'

Danda turned and plucked the ngwu agelega which he had planted beside the orange tree, and ran with it to another section of the crowd. The latter were greatly alarmed, cried out and turned to flee. But the ranks were too thick and they only fell against one another shrieking.

Danda spared them. Just before he reached the first rank he reined in and shouted:

'Kliklikli!'

'Yiii—'

'Kliklikli—'

'Yiii!'

Danda left them and ran to the next section. But here he met with a rebuff. For it was in this section that the chieftain of Aniocha and most of the ozo men sat. And they had seen Danda's ngwu agelega.

'Kliklikli—' shouted Danda again. Silence. Danda turned away, and ran. At the same time a young man with cowtail moustaches who had been whispering with the chieftain approached and drew him aside.

'What has happened to you?' Danda asked.

'Give me that ngwu agelega,' said the young man roughly. 'You are not fit.'

'The chieftain said you should give it me.'

Danda looked back and saw that the old man was taking a keen interest in the discussion. The music had stopped.

'No,' said Danda. 'It is not done.'

'Then you must leave the field,' said cowtail. 'The music cannot play as long as you are here.'

Danda pondered for a while and then said: 'It is well,' and began to move away.

And the drums started again singing.

CHAPTER THREE

'It is a small matter,' said an Uwadiegwu ozo.

'It is not a small matter,' an Ikolo man, name of Agali, countered sharply. 'If a man who is not an ozo handles the ngwu agelega it is not a small thing. It is an alu, Hoha!' He threw the last expression down like a gage.

But his opponents could not see the challenge for night had come down.

'Bring us the light, woman,' said a dry plaintive voice from the midst of the men.

A small girl came from one of the women's quarters carrying a large hurricane lantern. She placed it on a long massive table which ran the whole length of the room. The spluttering light discovered the room, a long narrow rectangle which seemed specially built for family gatherings. The numerous goats skulls which hung down from the ceiling must also have seen many meetings and their grins seemed to signify: 'What, another one!'

Silhouetted against the light and at the head of the table was the chieftain, a peevish looking man whose small, leathery face sprouted wisps of white hair. By his right sat his son, an impressive figure, light-complexioned, massive. Another man sat on the other side, a truculent individual with restless eyes, a short stocky figure and a disproportionately large head. The other ozos had arranged themselves on both sides of the table in places where they would expect to see and be seen.

'Don't muzzle me!' roared Agali though nobody wanted to. 'It is an alu,' he bristled. He was a burly figure cushioned with fat and carrying a barrel of a belly like a distinguished burden. Below the belly a small but rich cloth draped his extensive waist.

'When the son of Ejiofo used ozo parrot's feathers on his cap it was not a small thing. We fined him four baskets of

22

yam, four large pots of palm wine, a cow, a goat, a cock that has cried and two baskets of baked cassava. Which one of you was not there when we shared the prize among us. Ahai!' The last utterance was expressed in such a manner as to suggest both triumph and disgust.

'Everybody remembers the case,' said a youthful ozo slinging his cowskin bag from the arm where it rested to the shoulder. 'I knew young Chukwudi Ejiofo. The reason why we dealt harshly with him was that he was headstrong. He said to us that ozos cannot expect to own all the parrot's feathers in the world. Yes, he was a wild young man. When a criminal's face says that he is sorry for his crime, the judge swallows his own anger, but if the criminal stuffs his ears and binds his head with akwala string what mercy can he expect?'

'Did Danda's face say he was sorry?' cried Agali relentlessly. 'When Nwora Otankpa asked him to give the ngwu agelega Danda answered: "You are not fit." Abia! This last expression probably signified that people who disagreed with this particular ozo were stuttering.

'When I spoke to him he said that the ngwu agelega was his father's.'

'No man can hold on to what Danda says. What Danda says has neither head nor tail.'

There was laughter.

'It does not amuse me!' roared the Ikolo man. 'It is long since Danda began pouring sand into our eyes.'

'But is the ngwu agelega his or his father's? We want to know.'

All directed their several gazes at the truculent man with the large head. This ozo darted a sharp glance at the last speaker but said nothing. The ozos silently appealed to the chieftain but the chieftain was asleep. He always slept through such meetings but at the end people would be surprised at the amount of detail of the proceedings he remembered. Meanwhile Nwokeke, his son, assumed command.

'Araba,' he said to the big-headed ozo. 'Is the ngwu agelega yours?'

Araba stirred and said calmly: 'This is a question for

Danda himself. I haven't been home to know whether the ngwu agelega he carried is mine or his.'

'Why should he have one? Is he an ozo man?'

'His father is.'

'What do I hear? Do the laws say now that if a man's father is an ozo that man can carry an ngwu agelega? Or are you making new laws for us?' It was evident that something else other than Danda's indiscretion was eating Agali. And that thing soon came out. 'I know you, you Uwadiegwus,' continued he. 'You are full of tricks. You would defend your brother.'

The lion of family loyalties is always round the corner in his lair, baleful, red-eyed, prickly, easily roused. It is usually best to let him be. For once he is lured into the open there is no limit to his rampage. He will elbow aside the other characters in the drama and occupy the stage alone.

Now the issues were no longer between Danda and constituted authority but between the two principal family groups in Aniocha, the Ikolos and the Uwadiegwus. The Uwadiegwus took up the challenge at once.

'Danda springs from a big obi,' said Idengeli, one of the most influential of the Uwadiegwu ozos. 'When a rich man's son breaks the golden pot his father's barn will pay.'

'True word,' said another family man shaking hands with Idengeli. 'When Araba dies is it not Danda who will cover his outer walls, marry his women?'

'Was the father of young Chinedu Ejiofo not an ozo?' asked Agali. 'Was Ejiofo Omile not an ozo? But when his son grew a strong head we fined him four baskets of yams, four pots of palm wine, a cow, a goat, a cock that has cried and two baskets of cassava. Do you think we of the Ikolo umunna could not have defended him if we wanted to, since he was our brother?'

'Are we now to compare Araba's obi with Ejiofo Omile's? Have we lost a sense of what is proper?'

'Ejiofo Omile was the greatest ozo our land has seen. His barn would have fed the whole of Aniocha, man, woman, child—'

'Such a story has never entered my ear. This is the first time I am hearing it.'

'It is open-eyed truth. Truth that can face the light of day . . .'

'I have never heard it.'

'You are new to Aniocha then—'

It is possible that this family rivalry would have become sharper and sharper until all traces of the original purpose of the meeting had been lost. But just at this moment the old chieftain woke from his sleep.

'Nobody has said what we should do to Danda,' he said sensibly peering at the ozos, his eyes still hazy with sleep.

'We have decided,' said Idengeli, 'that his father should settle the matter with his son. Let him take away from him the ngwu agelega.'

'We have decided no such thing,' cried Agali. 'We—'

'Son of our fathers? . . .' The chieftain turned feebly to Araba.

'Troubles that started from Danda have broken my head,' said Araba. 'I don't know what to say.'

The chieftain summed up. 'He will give us four large pots of palm wine, four baskets of yams, a cow, a goat, a cock that has cried and two baskets of baked cassava—and then for the rest of the scorch season he is not to be seen in the ebe. If I know Danda,' murmured the chieftain cradling his face with his wan hands, 'if I know Rain that will break his heart.' The chieftain went back to sleep.

CHAPTER FOUR

'Troubles that started with Danda have broken my head,' repeated Araba as he reached his obi, a mud rectangular house helmeted with thatch, with two big pillars—

'Rain,' deprecated his companion, Okelekwu, a lean dog of a man silhouetted against the palm oil light. 'Which way has he taken now—'

Araba stood up, unslung from the nail on one of the pillars a small calabash topped by a gourd cup, sat down again, filled the cup and passed it to his guest. Okelekwu drank, smirked his lips and said: 'Strong Aniocha wine.'

'It is my brother, Diochi, who has tapped it. Diochi is the best tapster about these parts . . . I had wanted to ask Danda to tap our palms but that would be like sending the vulture to the market to go and buy you meat which is as much as asking it to go in to a feast. Danda would drink all the wine he taps and eat the calabash too—'

'True word,' replied Okelekwu in a sad deprecatory tone. Then with an old cowtail whisk which he always carried with him he swished away the moths which were obscuring the light.

'I used to think it was agwu but I don't think so now. Danda does everything he does with open eyes.'

'Ahai!'

'It is my misfortune . . . I have a weak Ikenga, I think.' Araba stared reproachfully at the largest of the family gods, a warlike image carrying a cutlass and fierce mien—

Okelekwu thought: 'Has he a weak Ikenga? . . . And there is his large barn and he is an ozo and has ten women. Has he a weak Ikenga?' But aloud he said: 'One's chi brings one so many troubles—'

'Why should my chi bring an akalogholi into my compound. Have I ever committed an alu? Did I sell a virgin into slavery? Have I ever slept with a widow?'

'Who will say so?'

'Danda is in the same age group as Nwora Otankpa. Let me see.' Araba counted on his fingers, but couldn't recollect how many years that was. 'Yes,' he said, 'in the same age group as Nwora Otankpa. They were born a year after the first locusts came. Nwora has settled down, has two women and makes his voice heard in Aniocha, but Danda, what has Danda done?'

Okelekwu shrugged his shoulders.

'He flutes!' shouted Araba. 'He flutes from the cry of the cock to the time the chicken return to roost . . . I don't say he shouldn't make music. In my time I sang with the flute and beat the drum. No man could dance the Ogwulugwu dance better. But a man cannot sing all day. A man should stand below the sun, should not bow down before the rain—'

'True word.' Okelekwu scratched his bottom and caressed the air with his cowtail whisk.

Araba dipped his hand into a cowskin bag hanging on the chair and brought out a snuff tin. He knocked this thrice on his knee, opened it and with a small snuff spoon made of bone he scooped some snuff into his nostrils sighing luxuriously. Then he gave the tin to Okelekwu. Okelekwu snuffed and sighed: 'It is fresh tobacco.'

For a moment Araba looked at the Ikenga then spoke more quietly than he had hitherto done.

'One has to think of those who will come after him. It will be the duty of Danda to thatch my outer walls after I am gone, to bury me. Can Danda bury me?'

'One can't say. He may be a different man after you are gone. A man I knew at Obeledu was a scamp, but as soon as his father was gone—'

'At Obeledu, you say,' said Araba scenting a story.

'Yes.'

'What was the man's name? I have friends at Obeledu.'

'Orakwue Akunnia . . . Yes, that was the name.'

'I don't know him.'

'His son, as I said, was a scamp . . . once he stole a cock from a neighbour. When they asked him about it he denied the theft. He said he was prepared to swear before the Alusi. His relatives nodded their heads and said they would take him to swear. The next day they all went to the shrine and there they found no Alusi. It had been stolen.'

'Ahai!'

'Yes. But the boy was not a scamp for long. As soon as his father, Orakwue, was laid into the earth the boy woke up, took over his father's wives and married them firmly. Now the outer walls of his compound are never bare.'

'It began early,' said Araba, who had not listened to the latter part of Okelekwu's story. 'He began to go to waste early. It is people of his age group who have read books,

27

know the ways of the white man and ride in land-boats. But in his boyhood he stuffed his ears to books. They used to buy them clothes and give them sweetmeats so that they would come to school. Danda would eat the meat but after that would run: sacham! into the bush. I used to laugh at his tricks then. Two of his brothers were attending school regularly and I said: "We cannot all be white men in this compound. Let Danda remain with me," I said, "and go to the shrine so that after his brothers would have gone to make money in the big towns he would keep my yam barn and wash the faces of my fathers clean." Now it looks as if he will lose both up and down.'

There was silence after this as each man followed his thoughts. 'That's how it is,' said Araba at last, blinking, for the snuff had brought tears to his eyes. 'My Ikenga was blind the day Danda was born.'

The darkness thickened and the palm oil light, stuck into a cassava step tripod, became brighter. Outside, the crickets had begun to chant briskly. From the women's quarters came sounds of animated life. Some babies cried and were hushed. A woman scolded her daughter very loudly.

Araba seemed to be preparing a weighty remark. After staring angrily at Okelekwu for a moment he made it. 'Danda will eat sand this scorch season.'

'How?'

'He is to give the Ozos four baskets of yams, four pots of palm wine, a cow, a goat, a cock that has cried, two baskets of baked cassava.'

'Ahai!'

Somewhere outside, the air was merry with tinkles. Araba sneezed passionately and cleaned his nostrils with the back of his left hand. Okelekwu waved the moths away.

The thick door of the gate banged violently open and Danda came in through it, singing. He was just about to go into his small hut which stood a few paces from the gate but Araba called him to the obi.

'How did you come about an ngwu agelega, Danda?'

'I made it.'

'Are you an ozo man?'

28

'No. But my father is.'

Araba said nothing to this.

Danda turned to Okelekwu and called his praise name:
'Nwayo bu ije'—slow be our journey.

'Rain,' Okelekwu had just served himself palm wine and
still carried the calabash.

'There is a little in it,' he answered.

'Let's have it then,' said Danda laughing. 'The Tortoise
once came into a friend's house. The friend had just finished his food. But he said to Tortoise: "You meet me as I
am just about to finish my meal." "Let's have the little that
remains," said Tortoise.'

He tipped the calabash into the gourd cup and drank.

Araba waited for him to finish and then said: 'People
in your age group are doing things, marrying, begetting
children, buying land-boats. What have you done?'

'Time is still big,' said Danda.

The answer exasperated Araba and for a moment he
said nothing, merely tapped on his knees. At last, 'And the
Ozos say you should pay them four baskets of yams, four
pots of palm wine, a cow, a goat, a cock that has cried,
two baskets of cassava.'

'Why?' asked Danda, shaken.

'And you are not to appear in the ebe for six moons.'

'Impossible.' Danda thought for a moment, finished the
second cup he had been carrying and continued:

'I will attend the next dance.'

'It is not wise,' said Okelekwu. 'A man who is sensible
does not, open-eyed, jump into the fire.'

'I will attend the next dance,' Danda said again.

Araba snuffed, sighed, and said:

'It is when a dog hungers for death that it begins to eat
sand.'

CHAPTER FIVE

Danda attended the next dance. This one was held to celebrate the death of the old chieftain. Danda had led it with his flute and afterwards had, with the third age group, raced round Aniocha killing bad spirits, cleaning the roads so that the journey of the spirit of the chieftain would be smooth. As soon as the rituals were complete, Danda, still smeared with white clay, made his way to the chieftain's compound. An Ikolo ozo met him just by the gate and drew him aside.

'Akunnia,' Danda praised him respectfully.

'Rain,' said the Ikolo ozo and then: 'You came to the ebe today.'

'True word.'

'Did your father not tell you of the chieftain's order?'

'True word. But we have settled all that. We met the chieftain many days ago and I bowed the knees to him and told him that I had erred. The chieftain said that it is well, that he would leave me off. He said when a criminal binds his head with akwala string and stuffs his ears he cannot expect any mercy. But when a criminal bows the knees and says biko then the judge swallows his anger.'

'Were the ozos present when the chieftain said this?'

'Yes.'

'Uwadiegwu ozos?'

'No, all the ozos of Aniocha.'

'I wasn't there,' said the Ikolo man angrily.

'Perhaps the messenger who was sent to call the ozos forgot you.'

'Forgot me! It is well.' The Ikolo man walked huffily away feeling very much slighted.

Danda moved off. He had not taken many steps before another ozo, this time an Uwadiegwu, met him.

'Danda,' this man said. 'You broke our order.'

'True word,' said Danda. 'We have settled all that.'

'How?'

'We, my father and me, met the chieftain many days ago and explained to him that the ngwu agelega I carried was not mine but my father's. The chieftain said very well that I was free but that I must be more careful next time. Oh, we have finished with the case.'

'Were the ozos present when the chieftain forgave you?'

'No, only my father and me were present.'

'It is well,' said the Uwadiegwu ozo, satisfied.

Danda went away to confront other ozos.

The Ikolo ozo had watched from a distance the conversation between Danda and the Uwadiegwu man. At its conclusion he approached his fellow noble.

'What does Danda say it is?'

'The chieftain has forgiven him.'

'So you were there. And nobody thought of sending for me. They forgot me,' the Ikolo man said bitterly.

'Who said I was there?'

'Were you not there?'

'No.'

'Danda said to me that everybody was there except me.'

'He told me that nobody was there except him and his father.'

'True word?'

'Do I say to you: "Don't tell another person"?'

'Ahai! You cannot get a hold on what Danda says. What Rain says has neither head nor tail. Let us go and see what is passing.'

The ozos had gathered in the long iron-roofed obi, and had broken into knots of two or three, whispering. In their midst stood an assortment of gifts, a cow being the chief one, as well as clay-pots of palm wine and an open box containing money. These were known as spirit gifts and were due to the ozos at the death of any of their member. Until they were satisfied with these gifts the body would not be buried. They were not satisfied. The money perhaps was adequate and so perhaps was the palm wine, 'but the cow, son of our fathers—? Ahai, days have passed when cows were plump and hulking. Think of the beast that was used for burying Ozo Ejiofo; it filled the mouth. But this one looks like a bundle of firewood. The world is changing. Things are getting worse and worse.'

Araba mediated. He made a long speech saying how easy it is to find fault with someone else's palm wine but how difficult it is to buy your own, and how hard things were nowadays what with tax and the price of things rising— His speech dampened the enthusiasm of cavillers but did not sway all the ozos. Many still insisted that the thin cow should be exchanged. Araba whispered with Nwokeke and the latter soon after that went into one of the women's quarters. He returned carrying a squawking rooster.

'See what he has brought us in addition people of our land,' said Araba. 'He has been a man.'

'Yes he has been a man,' shouted Idengeli. A few ozos still demurred but didn't want to press their objection. Besides, strong bubbling Aniocha wine was before them. They couldn't wait.

The umuokpu could and did wait. The umuokpu are the daughters of Aniocha married out to other towns. From early morning they had walked Aniocha roads, killing evil spirits with their short, blunt knives. Then they had visited the compounds of their friends and relatives. Many an Aniocha householder had avoided them and gone for some 'little business' at Eziakpaka or Mbammili. Those who had stayed in had paid with a smile. The women had left, singing praises to those that are open-handed and damning misers. Then they had come to the chieftain's compound, received their own gifts, whispered about them, were dissatisfied and said so. 'The cocks had not cried, the ewe dropped, was it sick or what?'

For an hour Nwokeke cajoled them but did not get far. So he tried to see what he would achieve by bribing their leaders. One of the most influential was Araba's sister married into Mbammili. Nwokeke persuaded Araba to speak to her.

Brother and sister seldom saw eye to eye. In fact for

months before this they had not been on speaking terms. Now, however, they were forced to forget their rancour in the interest of the honour of the Uwadiegwu kindred.

After a perfunctory greeting, they began to talk about matter close to their hearts: the progress of the woman's two sons and Danda's disturbing knavery. Only then did they start on what had brought them together.

'It is women from the other umunnas who have bound their heads with akwala string over this affair,' said Araba. 'You shouldn't allow them to soil things for us.'

'I know,' said the sister. 'We will shut their mouths . . . But, Araba, they tell me that when the umuokpu came to your house you gave only two shillings. Were you not ashamed?'

'Two shillings was enough. Is it not long since they began eating me?'

'Two shillings? My mouth closed when I heard it.'

'I cannot dress the umuokpus with my money all my life.'

'Two shillings! It was not like you.'

'Did they want to carry me with them?'

'Since I left Aniocha none of my brothers has ever done anything that would make me proud.'

'It is the way you talk—'

Brother and sister had parted with mutual disregard. Still the crisis was not to be resolved. Eventually the women won their point. A fiery rooster was substituted for the tepid one and a new ewe was offered, now fighting-fit.

The sun had reached his home in Mbammili and was now about to sink into its waters. The chieftain, preceded by the emblems of his rank and followed by volleys of dane-guns, went home with the red deity. Aniocha rejoiced. There were to be three market weeks of dancing, feasting, merry-making. Relatives once more gathered from the neighbour-ing towns. Once more there was loud laughter in the nights and children, their mouths oily oily, ran around the lanes blowing the crops of chicken to make balloons.

The man on whom the heaviest burden lay was Nwokeke

Idemmili.. At the end of the third market week he was to call the whole of Aniocha 'to carry in and drink'; that is, every man was to bring to the feast a pot of wine and in return was to be fed by the host and given some yams to carry home to his family.

Nwokeke did himself well and won the esteem of everybody. Many said the old chieftain had cause to feel proud of the fruit of his loins.

'It is not having a son that counts, it is having one that can bury you well.'

'True, indeed.'

Idemmili returned to his obi on the seventh market week, accompanied by the dread Ojionu. There was great fear and trembling all over the compound as it was known that the spirits had risen. Women ran into the inner rooms of their houses and huddled close with their whimpering children. A terrible silence prevailed. The two spirits at first walked all over the yard looking searchingly at different corners to make sure that all was well. The Ojionu touched a coconut and it began to wither. Then they came into the obi where some men sat. Without taking any notice of the latter they squatted before the Ikenga and drank the palm wine which had been left them at its foot. The Uwadiegwus remained tense, their heads bent to the ground. Not a sound was heard from them to disturb the comfort of those two immortals. At last the spirits had done, rose and went back to the land of the spirits.

Danda bade them farewell with his flute. He sang about some Aniocha hero who had been caught in an ambush at Eziakpaka.

'I am singing about the days when the world was young,' Danda began. 'Do you hear me, Okeke Ugo.'

'Hai!' shouted Okeke Ugo, a tall rawboned fellow. And he rose, spreading his hands wide as if he were preparing to fight, his body trembling . . . 'Hai, things have spoilt—'

'A big man falls in battle, when there is another he is remembered.' The notes of the oja acquired colour and movement. The ambush was laid. The warriors rode into the night carrying long spears and surrounded the sleeping

warrior. He fell to them but not until a dozen warriors had
been sent to the land of the spirits.

'Hai!' roared Okeke Ugo as the notes trailed to the end.
Then he crumbled and wept.

CHAPTER SIX

The Ozo men were now to choose a new chieftain and at
first it seemed they were in for an easy task. It wouldn't
be like the last election when so many bad words had passed
between Ikolo and Uwadiegwu and so much ogwu thrown
about for the purpose of influencing the minds of opponents. Then, there had been problems of procedure to be
settled and about this there had been as many opinions
as there were ozos or even commoners in Aniocha. This
time the steps to be followed were plain. Seven market weeks
after the death of the last chieftain candidates to fill the
vacancy were to be called for from all the families. Then
the ozos would meet, and voting secretly, select the most
suitable.

And there was little doubt who it would be. Araba. His
father had ruled before Idemmili. He had many other
qualifications: a long barn, ten women, an obi of which
much noise was made. Araba was known too to have
always been a fighter for Aniocha and Uwadiegwu. Finally
and most important of all, he had taken the ozo before
anybody alive. One couldn't have stronger claims to the
recognition than precedence. There were people, though,
who had misgivings about Araba's qualities as a ruler. They
feared his arrogance and his partiality for litigation. He had
taken many people to the village court and what is more
had in most cases triumphed. Many called him 'that big
head' referring both literally to the size of the top of his
body and metaphorically to the size of his pride. So it
seemed to them that if he became chieftain he would be
open-handed—one was always sure of a cup of wine in

Araba's compound—and honest—'Araba hasn't two mouths,' people said, 'when he said yes it was yes'—but he would also be stern and uncompromising and always at logger-heads with the ozos.

It would be better if Araba gave up his claims to the son of the last chieftain. Nwokeke was more amiable, though no man's fool, and open-handed too. He had been one of the first policemen employed by the white man. And it was perhaps from this job that he had acquired his skill in administration, for the first policemen had been sharp intriguers. It was from that employment, too, that he had made his money. A few years after he had returned to Aniocha he had entered the ozo and built an iron house in his compound. He hadn't as many women or as long a barn as Araba but he kept an open house and fed his kindred often.

There was little fear though that the Uwadiegwu front would be split by the rivalry between its chief sons, for Nwokeke had given out that he was backing Araba. So the umunna could face their chief opponents in unity.

The Ikolo were determined to wrest the prize from the hands of the Uwadiegwus; it had been with the latter for four generations. They knew they couldn't match them in number—the Uwadiegwu had more ozos than the other umunnas put together—but at least they could employ the weapon of the weak; guile. They had found out that certain Uwadiegwu ozos were in need of money. The Ikolos, men and women, subscribed it and bought the needy ozos' votes. In addition they made some ogwus which would pour sand into Uwadiegwu eyes and make them act in opposition to their deepest instincts—vote for aliens.

The ogwu worked. Two days later it was reported that the white District Officer would come to visit Aniocha. In the absence of a chieftain somebody was required to stand out and welcome the white man to Aniocha: Ozo Agali, an Ikolo man, was chosen to do it. And that night it seemed to some people that the sound of the pestle on Ikolo mortar was a trifle louder than usual.

The Uwadiegwu ozos appeared nervous when they met in Araba's obi. They all tried to speak at once. Somebody in rising tipped the palm wine down the cloak of Idengeli, but Idengeli was too excited to take notice.

'It is ogwu they have made us, strong ogwu.'

'There are tortoises in our midst.'

'Snakes!'

'Nothing will spoil,' said Araba after the wave of excitement had calmed. 'We must swear the oath. It is the only thing that will save us.'

They rose, threw their cloaks over their shoulder, and walked up to the shrine. And there each man swore before the Alusi that he would not fail his own side.

When next week the ozos met to elect a chieftain all the Uwadiegwus stood behind Nwokeke. And he won. And in this way he became both the Chief of Aniocha as well as the head of the Uwadiegwu kindred.

CHAPTER SEVEN

'You have unfortunate legs,' said Araba welcoming his visitors. 'I have just finished morning food.'

They thanked him.

'But you shall have that which you have met.' He poured palm wine into a gourd cup and served the older of the two men. Nwobu Esili, a mite of a man with sharp features and a cringing manner, drank, fidgeted, and looked round furtively. Nwora Otankpa tossed off his own cup at a gulp, smirked his lips and remarked:

'Strong aniocha, but I have drunk stronger.'

'Let me give you another cup, Nwobu.'

'You have done well,' said Nwobu.

'No, we are in a hurry,' roared the younger man. 'Don't serve him again.'

But Araba ignored this order and served Nwobu.

'Well, now, it is about this message,' continued the young man. 'The chieftain wants everybody in his obi this morning.'

'Why wasn't the ogene man sent round?' asked Araba. 'People no longer listen to the ogene,' said Nwora. 'And even if they listened they would say they didn't. They would leave for their farms and when you asked them "Why didn't you come to the meeting?" they would say "I didn't hear the ogene." So the chieftain has asked us to go and tell everybody by mouth.'

'What shall we talk about? Did Nwokeke'—Araba hadn't yet got used to calling Nwokeke the chieftain—'did he tell you what we shall talk—'

'He didn't, but is it hard to guess? I ask you is it hard to guess?' Nwora Otankpa spoke always with a shout, with violent gestures, his cowtail moustache bristling. Among people who knew him well he was called 'kill and trample'. 'Many things have been spoiling in our umunna. Men sleep with widows, others make nsi to stop other people's wives from delivering. Can you ask me what there is to talk about?'

'Does Nwobu know?'

'Ah!' said Nwobu staring at the roof and rubbing down his adam's apple, 'hear what you ask. He! he! he! How should I know what the chieftain thinks? I know my place he! he! he! As Danda would say: "If a child begins to wear clothes before he is fit for them the wind will bear him away clothes and all." ' Nwobu continued for long to relish the joke in silence.

Nwora Otankpa was already shouting: 'What we have to talk about is many . . . Yes, the chieftain says, for instance, that you have the ozala of the umunna. Have you the umunna ozala?'

Araba nodded. 'What about it?'

'The chieftain wants it. It should be in his obi.'

Araba said nothing more.

'That's how it is,' said Nwora rising. 'Come, Nwobu, let's go.'

'Tell Nwokeke that the ozala will remain here,' said

Araba. 'It is well,' said Nwobu.

Nwora Otankpa was already near the gate. 'Kill and trample,' Araba murmured. He approved of Nwora Otankpa. True, the latter was bumptious but his bumptiousness was an expression of his restless energy. Nwora was rising fast. Young as he was he already had two wives and was preparing for the ozo. Araba wished Danda were made of the same stuff.

After his visitors had gone Araba climbed on to a wooden seat and stretching his hand to the grass mat which stretched across the roof, serving as a sort of ceiling, he brought down a heavy ivory trumpet. This was the umunna ozala. Every ozo man had an ozala but the Uwadiegwu umunna had a special one which had served them both as a standard and a herald. It was now sooty and cobwebbed from disuse. Araba took a rag and cleaned it carefully. Then he put his mouth to its speaking hole and called the praise name of his father; omekokwulu—one who does what he says. The round mellow hoot of the ozala brought forcefully to his memory the great moments of his father's life: the triumphant appearances on days when the great men of Aniocha took titles, the yearly visits to the white District Officer when Udeji was accompanied by a troupe of praise singers and umbrella-bearers. On many of these occasions Araba had carried the umunna ozala.

After the death of Udeji the headship of Aniocha and so of the Uwadiegwus had passed to Idemmili. But one of the symbols of his authority, the ozala, had remained in the Udeji obi. The old chieftain had been so powerful that many people still looked to his house for leadership. Perhaps that was why Nwokeke called for the ozala. He would be determined not only to take power but to maintain all its symbols. Araba would forestall him. If he couldn't have the chieftaincy which Nwokeke had usurped by guile he would hold on to the ozala. He knew he could count on the support of a great many people. Okekekwu could be trusted to make a persuasive speech. Idengeli . . . it was difficult to know which side Idengeli would be on. He had often been one of Araba's formidable opponents in the

39

umunna but Araba knew him well enough to be sure that that wouldn't sway his judgment. Then there was Nwora Otankpa. He was one of Nwokeke's young men and would definitely shout against Araba. But then he was only on the fringe of, not within that exclusive circle of influence formed by grey hairs and Ozos. The danger from him as yet had little bite.

The sun had begun to warm the earth. Araba picked off from a nail on a pillar a woollen shirt, a present from his son who worked in the city, and put it on over a stiff wrapper that encircled the waist and reached the ankles. Then he put on a brownish helmet plumed with three flaming parrot's feathers. His dressing was completed by a cowskin bag which was slung over his right shoulder trailing down the side. Confident of the impression he would make he bowed through the narrow passage between the low roof and the ojo, plucked his ngwu agelega from the ground and set out.

A signpost stood in front of the compound facing the main road and a notice written in bold characters was pasted on it. Araba's first impulse was to pull the post down—the man who put it there should have informed him before doing so—but he resisted the desire, perhaps the sign was put up there by the white man. Then, too, there was a mystery about paper and ink which inspired awe.

Two small boys were playing football in a lane, using yam sticks taken from a nearby farm as goal posts.

'Come here,' Araba shouted.

One of them walked briskly up to him.

'What is your name?'

'Mathew.'

'Eh?'

'Mathew.'

'It is well,' said Araba giving up the attempt to say it. 'Look at this paper. Is it from the white man? You learn such things in school.'

'It is Nweke Alusi,' said the boy.

Araba snorted. He knew Nweke Alusi and didn't like him very much. They said his ogwu was powerful but Araba

40

would rather go to the old dibias than to Nweke Alusi who was noisy and mercenary and, Araba was sure, unreliable.

'What does he say?'

The poster read:

'Nweke Alusi, native doctor.

Registered in Nigeria.

Man-pass-Man!

Come to me for power medicine—Tó kure madness, hatfelior, "akpu" foming in the maut (epilezi), venerable diseasis e.t.c. Money back if not satisfactri.

Come for India talisman and rings to help you pass examination.

Love medicine—If your wife runs away come to me. I will bring her back—come one, come all!' The poster was decorated with a skull and cross-bones.

The boy first read it in English then translated.

'Wait,' said Araba. 'If my wife runs away from me Nweke Alusi will bring her back?'

'That's what it says here.'

'Stuttering,' muttered Araba pulling up the post and throwing it into the copse nearby, 'if my wife runs away I don't need ogwu to bring her back. I will go to her parents and ask for my bride price.'

About half of the umunna were already waiting in the Idemmili compound. Most ozo men sat on stools but commoners were content with mats and goat-skins spread on the ground.

All greeted Araba as he came in and called his praised name, Nwokeke, smiling, waved him on to a chair near his own. Araba greeted the new chieftain, sat down and looked about, and saw that Idengeli was next to him.

'What do they say it is?' he asked him.

'We have not yet been told,' answered Idengeli extending his snuff box to Araba. 'There is a rumour that we will bind ourselves before the Alusi.'

'Something fit to be done. There is far too much alu being done nowadays.'

They waited. Occasionally somebody would mutter: 'Ahai, what is keeping them? The sun will soon reach the middle.' Others would snort in agreement. But they were not really angry. Punctuality is not one of the virtues of the Aniocha man. He takes time over his snuff and his palm wine and if you attempted to hurry him from either he would excuse himself by reminding you of the proverb: where the runner reaches there the walker will reach eventually.

When I make an appointment with an Aniocha man I have to make allowance for his way of looking at time. I do not ask him to meet me at the fourth striking of the clock. I tell him to come in the evening, and leave him one of three choices: just at the time the sun is beginning to set; after it has set; in the night.

More people were drifting in now and usually in a breezy manner. Danda was one of the last to come and he greeted the umunna with typical ebullience:

'Kliklikli!'
'Yiii!'
'Kliklikli!'
'Rain!'
'If there is any one to whom what is good is not good let him embrace the thorn tree and see how he likes it.'

The feeling of animation which he had helped to create persisted until Nwokeke rose to speak.

'People of our land, I greet you . . . I give to each man his due. Our day is good again. Isn't our day good again? I was small, just about this height when Uwadiegwu rose to be king. And since then the kingship has remained in his obi. It will continue to remain there . . . Let them all come. Let them, let Ikolo gnash their teeth but they won't pull us. By the help of those who are in the ground we shall remain on top, people of my family. But we must love each other. Let no man carry nsi. Every man must be able to look up; the man who looks down is an alu man, people of our land. Yes, the man who doesn't know his kindred is dead. The greatest of all words is the word "mine" and it is a fool who does not know this . . .' The rest of the speech was spun out with proverbs and tended to the same point.

Then for a moment there was silence as each man prepared his own speech. At last Nwora Otankpa bawled impatiently:

'Let us talk what it is we have to talk and be done with it.'

'True word,' agreed Nwokeke, looking at Nwora curiously. The young man was getting out of hand, taking too much on himself. Still Nwokeke rose again and became more explicit than he had so far been. There were important matters that had jumped out but first there was an old one to be cleared. 'The time for Mgbafo Ezira has come.'

She was a lengendary heroine of the Uwadiegwu umunna. The story had it that she had been a widow of Mbammili who had seven sons. At the time of the slave trade she was harried by slave raiders but had fought them back. At last she could fight no longer and fled to Aniocha for refuge. The Uwadiegwus sheltered her. But even here she could not escape her fate. One night slave raiders broke into her house, killed her and took away her children. The Uwadiegwus were furious and vowed revenge on the criminals but when they went to a dibia the afa said that the murderers of Mgbafo Ezira were Uwadiegwus. So from that time, the kindred had yearly sacrificed a cow to clean their honour and lay the ghost of the wronged woman.

'And listen to me!' shouted Nwora Otankpa. 'We buy that cow with money. The nama do not give it to us of their mercy. Last year I was sent to collect your money and I had a bad time. "My wife has fever, son of our fathers".'—Nwora mimicked the querulous tone of recalcitrants—'or "many of my children are in school, and tax has gone up." But I ask you, are we to buy the cow or not? And see here, let there be no question of churchman or non-churchman. The people who killed Mgbafo Ezira may have been the fathers of those who go to church today. Their descendants cannot hope to escape their own part of the shame by joining the white man.'

The church wouldn't contest the point. They had argued about it many times and it seemed futile to go on. So one of the members accordingly said that if they had known what the subject for the meeting would be they would not have come. As it was they couldn't stay. And with that he strode out followed by all the Christians.

'We will deal with them,' said Nwora. But this threat obviously was futile, it had no head. Three people out of ten cannot deal with seven, and the Christians outnumbered the pagans by an even greater proportion.

'Things have spoilt,' said Idengeli. And this note of resignation was echoed in the snuff sighs of the umunna. A messenger came at this point to say that the Alusi was ready. The men rose uneasily to face it. But Nwokeke stopped them.

'Wait, people of my land,' he said. His face was urgent, his manner dramatic.

The umunna settled down again.

'There are people who for long have condemned the umunna and the umunna has borne their insolence. But this time the umunna will speak up!' Nwokeke waited to see the effect his speech had. Many men looked about for the culprits. Then Nwokeke continued, turning to Araba:

'Son of our fathers, did you bring the ozala of the umunna!'

Araba's truculent, bloodshot eyes flamed but he said nothing.

'That's how it is, people of my land,' said Nwokeke smiling at the men.

This was the main object of the meeting. Nwokeke was not sure that his authority was complete. There was a small margin of uncertainty which he needed to clarify. That loyalty which people still owed to the Udeji house must be severed.

At first there were discreet murmurs. People were not yet sure which side to take.

At last Okelekwu rose. And one could sense a stir of expectation in the kindred. Okelekwu was one of the great speakers of the umunna. He was not a ranter. He didn't shout, he hadn't an impressive manner or delivery. He spoke quietly, smoothly, like a clear stream murmuring confidently on its way. He began with three choice proverbs all so perfectly appropriate to the matter that the umunna

44

marvelled again at the man's virtuosity. Then he rolled on, relaxed, an artist, unfolding the pleats of the garment of speech with a sure hand. At the end the men nodded with pleasure. True, it was difficult indeed to decide for whose cause he had been, he may or may not have edged slightly to Araba's side. No one could be sure. But did it matter? He had entertained them as they had seldom been entertained. The umunna sighed. They had eaten bitter-leaf of rare palate.

A small wispy herdsman next rose. He must tell the umunna the truth, Okelekwu had said all he himself had wanted to say. 'He has taken words from my mouth and I have nothing more to say.'

'Sit down then!' shouted many who were ready with their own speeches.

'But,' continued the herdsman, 'there is just one small bit—very small bit—which I wish to add.'

'Add it then.' Umunna faces were sceptical.

The herdsman did not add that small bit. He spent a long time trying to, but at the end had not quite succeeded. He said point by point what Okelekwu had said though of course he did not say it quite so well.

'I am not afraid of any one,' Nwora had been shouting. 'If Araba binds his head with akwala string we will deal with him!'

There were angry murmurs. Nwora had gone too far.

'Yes,' persisted the young man.

But the collective voices of the umunna bore him down. They talked. Everybody talked. The discussion had started when the sun was up in the middle. Now that same sun had almost reached the door of his home but still the umunna talked. Many people repeated themselves when they got the chance.

Now some were becoming impatient and crying out. But perhaps they only complained because they themselves were not making a speech. A palm wine tapper, for instance, had for a long time tried to stop more people from speaking. He didn't succeed, so he got up himself.

'My bottom is hot,' he cried. 'How long are we going

to stay here? People get up and talk and talk as if they were never going to make an end. Is there a law that a man must be long-winded? Is there any alu in being brief? If you have nothing to do, I have. My palms are waiting for me!'

The rest of the umunna nodded their heads in support. But the tapster having now cleared the ground, and created sympathy for himself, went ahead and made the longest speech of all.

At last it seemed the umunna was exhausted. Many faces were turned to the chieftain and he himself was about to sum up. But somebody rose before him: a big man with a round fresh-coloured face and eyes very genial but none too clever.

'Sit down,' many cried . . . But others who knew there were possibilities for comic relief in Nwafo Ugo only grinned.

'I won't sit down,' said the amiable giant. 'Many have spoken but I have not spoken. Why? Have those other people stronger arms than I have? Longer barns? More women? When the call for war is given in the dawn do they come out before me? Then why must they speak and I keep dumb?'

'You will speak, son of our fathers,' said the chieftain enjoying the situation.

'Speak, speak,' said the umunna between splutters of mirth.

Nwafo Ugo spoke. And the umunna were once again forced to listen to much that was obvious and inane.

Nwokeke didn't sum up this time but waited first to hear the opinion of someone whose voice told. Araba was pleased to see Idengeli rise. But at the same time Nwora Otankpa was up.

'Listen to me!' said Nwora.

'No, you listen to me,' said Idengeli harshly.

'I have been on my leg,' growled Nwora bending his shaggy brows on the ozo.

'Listen to me, Araba,' said Idengeli ignoring the young man who sat down, muttering angrily.

46

'I shall tell you word, Araba,' said Idengeli. 'I am not afraid of you. Why should I be? Do you feed me? Do I come to your house to beg for yam? My name is Idengeli. Ask in Aniocha and they will tell you that I am one that fears neither spirit nor man. Then who are you that I should be afraid to tell you word? Go and sit down! Listen to me. You will do what the chieftain tells you to do. This umunna will have only one head. Is that not our word, people of our land?'

'E-o-o-o!' chorused the umunna.

The matter was shelved. For when the umunna said 'E-o-o-o!' in that way it meant that they were tired of speeches and eager to go home. Nwokeke let them. But they only reached the path that led to his compound and settled down again.

The Alusi stood before them, a conelike god dressed in skins, blood and leaves. His priest was a tall, lanky man, who carried a twenty-year sore festering in his leg. He was dressed in a very dark cloak and his eyes were rounded with white clay. He looked fearful and was, in fact, the most feared man in Aniocha.

'You will come one by one,' he said in a dry, indifferent voice, 'and swear. And I need not tell you to speak the truth . . .'

There was no great eagerness in the men to come. For the Alusi is a ruthless killer, and destroys not only the home of those who have sworn falsely by it, but the homes of their umunna.

Nwokeke swore first. After him came Araba who digressed from the formula of the oath taking. He first referred to those who spoke with two mouths, then to people who hid their malice in their black hearts and carried deadly nsi with them. 'I like to meet my enemies in the open. Let them come out then and face me instead of carrying hidden nsi. Alusi, if I ever make nsi against a brother lay me low, if I call in a dibia against any human being lay me low, if out of envy I throw nsi about to prevent somebody's wife from delivering safe lay me low—'

Everyone had sworn now but for one man, a gaunt

47

fellow with a goatee; bright, lazy, eyes; who smoked a long, slightly charred pipe.

His name was Akumma Nwego and he was the most notorious loafer in the whole umunna. From morning till night he was to be seen on the ogwe at the motor-park chatting with other idlers or in the ebe drinking palm wine. Solitude did not bother him. He would often stay alone for hours turning up his toes and pulling at his pipe. Happily he had no one to support. His wife had died some years before leaving no issue. He had a younger brother, Nnoli, Danda's friend; but this one had since evolved his own style of self-survival. So Akumma had only himself to see to. And it had for long been a mystery how he did it. True, he made sure he attended all funeral celebrations but these could not keep his flesh firm, his eyes bright and his pipe alight all the year. It was generally agreed that whatever else Akumma fed on came out of other people's barns. In the gossip and imagination of the Uwadiegwus therefore he figured as a wily rogue, one who is too clever ever to be caught. It was not surprising that he would wish to escape the clutches of the Alusi. Nwora Otankpa forestalled him.

'Akumma Nwego,' he called. 'You have not sworn. Yes, look at me if you like, you have not sworn.'

'I have.'

'You have not,' some shouted truculently, others only amused at his effrontery.

Akumma Nwego surprised the umunna again. He rose and walked to the Alusi. And swore that he had never nor would ever take what did not belong to him, that he would never go in to somebody's widow, carry nsi, or make an ogwu to prevent an umunna man from making a success of any endeavour. Then with firm steps and a most serene countenance he walked back to his seat and resumed his charred pipe. Akumma Nwego was a cynic.

CHAPTER EIGHT

Stories had been going about that Danda had become a churchman.

'Which Danda is this?'

'How do you mean which Danda? There is only one Danda in this world.'

'Rain?'

'He.'

'Impossible!'

It had started with a visit groups of preachers made to various compounds. The churches were now taking steps to bring the last of the pagans into their fold. The group that visited Danda consisted of the catechist and a tall thin woman of great earnestness. Danda was returning from the market when he saw them emerge from the women's quarters where they had gone to preach. He greeted the catechist with fervour.

'Is this your face, Okoye Eze?' he shouted. 'What do you want with my father's wives? Back at your old tricks, are you?'

'Rain,' the catechist roared back.

They shook hands and laughed loud and long. At last Danda, still holding the catechist's hand, led the visitors to his hut and settled them on raised mud in the porch in front of the hut.

'Let's see whether Araba has some oji.' He walked over to the obi and brought from it a calabash of palm wine. He served the catechist and when the latter had drunk he took the cup and filled it for the woman.

'I don't drink,' she said.

'True word?' said Danda sipping. 'Have you heard the story how one day my grandfather, Udeji Uwadiegwu, asked somebody to come and drink wine. And that friend said no, and my grandfather said: "I will not take you before the

Alusi and get you to promise to drink with me!"'

The catechist smiled showing a speck of bitter-leaf soup which stuck to his uneven teeth.

'Well, and what is passing?'

The catechist finished his cup, smirked his lips, and said: 'You have not joined the church. Danda.'

'Is it my turn yet? My father is still out of it.'

'Everybody is joining,' said the woman. 'At Eziakpaka there is even a rush.'

'Time is running away,' said the catechist.

'Well suppose I join, what do I gain?'

'You gain eternal life,' said the woman.

'Your story is bent,' said Danda. 'Stretch it.'

'Our mother the church teaches that the world is not our home,' said Okoye Eze. 'We are like travellers who lodge in a place for a night and then move on. We are like the leaves of the plants, which are plucked in the morning and wither by night and die. When we mount to the sky we shall face the Lord who will say to good men: "Come ye, beloved of my father, possess the kingdom prepared for you," and to bad men: "Depart from me and get into the fire of the spirits." In which group will you be, Danda, which?'

'I will be with the good men, of course, hai!'

'Then you must join the church.'

'You do not need bright clothes to be a churchman. You can come in anything,' said the woman.

She was anticipating the excuse many pagans offered for not coming into the church—the lack of suitable garments with which to do so. After speaking with all the pagans of Aniocha she had come to the conclusion that almost every one of them would want to belong. The church had now come to be a prestige society, like the ozo. But just as no one would want to buy the ozo rank until he was fit, in the same way it seemed unseemly to get into the church before one had reached a certain stage in the social heights. The church was new and class, and one shouldn't enter it with anything but what was new and up-to-date. Accordingly most pagans, especially the women among them, would stay out until they had collected the bride price of their daughters or until their sons had obtained a government job. Then they could join the church in style.

'The church teaches humility, it is not the place for showing off or for finery,' the woman assured Danda.

'If you must follow me you must bear my cross,' said the catechist. He had just finished his third cup and was preening his black grippery shirt of the drop of wine which had perched on it. Okoye Eze was known as a man who loved his cups and this had endeared him to Aniocha men. His short rotund figure with the genial balding forehead was almost as familiar in Aniocha roads as Danda's be-belled own, and whenever he jangled past on his ancient bicycle, he was hailed all along the way. He was specially a favourite with the women, four of whom he kept, beside his wife. Okoye Eze was a man of great ability too and for many years had enjoyed complete authority in our church.

He spoke fast, his words coming in a steady unimpeded stream. With his fund of anecdotes and his genius for mimicry he was one of the greatest preachers our church has ever seen. Which one of us can ever forget his dramatization of a scene in hell catching just the right tone of agony and doom, or the incident in which after he had spoken passionately against the wave of licentiousness that was sweeping through Aniocha, two girls who had done something or the other the previous night had run out of the church in tears?

'Think of the day of your death, Danda. Now you are strong and fresh but what will you be tonight? What will the strongest of men, the most beautiful of women be? The King of the world in the morning and then chololom! Food for white ants in the evening.

'But as long as we are ready to meet our Lord nothing will spoil. Our sins have been swept away when God sent His only son to save us from the alu committed by our first parents. May the souls of the faithful departed—'

'Through the mercy of God rest in peace.'

The catechist next spoke of the passion of our Lord and

re-enacted the whole scene before Danda. At the end of the performance he asked:

'If you suffered for the world would you not expect gratitude?'

'Why suffer for the world?' Danda asked.

'Well, because you love them so well. And your suffering will save them from doom.'

'When I suffer from the world,' said Danda, 'they smile in my face but as soon as my back is turned they shrug their shoulders and say. "Don't take notice of Danda. He is no good." '

'And what then do you do?'

'Then I don't suffer for the world again.'

'That's it. Our Lord doesn't do that. He has suffered for men and men have turned their backs on Him and followed other gods and committed alu but He has not given the world up. Praise ye the Lord—'

'For His mercy abideth for ever . . .' added the woman.

'Now will you join the children of God, Danda? There is no time to lose. For the world is about to come to an end. Nation has risen against nation and brother has turned against brother. When you see the ogbu tree shed its leaves—'

The catechist had since formed the habit of breaking off in the middle of a biblical quotation and allowing his audience to finish it. In the present instance the woman said:

'Know ye that the scorch season has come.'

'I will join,' said Danda suddenly.

'Great one,' said Okoye Eze.

The two of them shook hands and looked appreciatively into each other's eyes.

But the woman was sceptical. She was a hardened campaigner—more than twenty people had joined the church after she had spoken to them—and knew the men. They told you airily that they would come but didn't.

Danda came. The next Sunday he jingled merrily into the church. Throughout the service the eyes of the people were more often on him than on the officiating white priest.

At the end curious spectators surrounded him.

'Each man to his own,' said Danda shaking hands all round. 'I have come to taste that thing you have been tasting.'

'Welcome, Danda,' they chorused.

The parish priest, Father Royde, who lived at Aniocha, had been intrigued by Danda's bells. He now asked the catechist:

'Who is he?'

'Rain, the singer,' said an elder.

'A well-known person?'

'His name makes noise.'

'It was me who brought him in,' said the catechist. He walked up to Danda and said to him: 'The fada wants to know you.'

'True word?' said Danda oblivious of the honour done him.

'Come along then,' said the catechist.

'His name is Danda, fada,' said the catechist, rubbing his balding head.

'Welcome,' said the priest in Ibo.

'Welcome, white man,' said Danda, suggesting by the inflection of his voice that the white man's accent could be bettered.

The spectators who had been milling around them smiled. And that was how the story spread:

'Did they use ogwu on him?' asked the giant, Nwafo Ugo.

'That is what I have been asking,' mused Okelekwu.

'I don't trust that white fada of theirs. I see him often walking the roads reading the ground and greeting no one. Is he not somebody to be feared?'

'White men have ogwu,' said a tapster. 'But nobody knows what the ogwu is like.'

The second and third age groups of the Uwadiegwu umunna were gathered just outside the compound of Nwokeke. They carried knives, axes and shovels. It was their turn to tidy the umunna footpaths. Many people were still to come so the early ones waited meanwhile and passed the news of the day. Akumma Nwego lit his charred pipe.

'But let me ask, people of our land,' Nwafo Ugo said, returning to Danda. 'Do you think Rain will miss the Mgbafo Ezira feast?'

'He won't,' said Nwora Otankpa with conviction.

'If he does then things must really have spoilt,' said Okelekwu, swishing away a thick swarm of sandflies.

A moment later the tinkle of bells announced Danda and he soon made his appearance.

Everybody looked at him with curiosity.

'Is it true you have now become a white man, Danda?' Nwafo Ugo asked.

'True word.'

'I greet you then.'

'Is the work finished?' asked Danda.

'Eee,' said Nwafo ironically. 'You can now go home and take Ekeama Idemmili's bitter-leaf soup.'

Some of the other men guffawed.

'Then stir up,' said Danda. 'Have your bones rusted?'

'You have just come.'

'Let's be about it, men of our lands. The day is dying. Hoa!'

'He hasn't even a hoe,' said Nwafo. But Danda had his flute. With this he fluted a work song. The Uwadiegwus stirred and rose. One or two jumped up and cried: 'Oi! oi! oi! I hear the voice of the flute.' And soon all were working at the lane with great verve.

They made much of Danda at the church. Father Royde was convinced that his conversion would attract other pagans. So he made the catechist appoint a special teacher to teach him the catechism. Danda learnt quickly. In a few days he knew who made him, why he was made, and other things. He could even sing some of the church songs with his oja. It would not be long, the catechist hoped, before he was baptized. But before this took place Danda came into serious conflict with the Church. He missed a church

54

service. That day he had been invited to a 'bring in and drink' ceremony at Mbammili and he had gone to it instead of to church.

To miss mass in the eyes of the church was a mortal sin punishable in heaven as well as on earth. For it was usually the first sign of apathy and the church needed to deal severely with this situation or they would lose most of their new members.

The converts at first showed great enthusiasm, they wore their new Sunday clothes with pride and learnt all that was to be learnt. In a few months' time as the novelty wore off they lost interest and grumbled at some of the church rules which were to them irksome. A man was not allowed more than one wife. Then what were the people who came into the church after marrying many wives to do? Put the others away, said the church. But then how was one to recover the bride price? The parents of the wife would have spent all of it. Then it frequently happened that a man's missis failed to give one an issue. One couldn't very well, if one could help it, resign oneself to the situation of dying without perpetuating one's line.

In many other ways the church failed to satisfy the converts. They said for instance that you shouldn't use ogwu. Then how was one to protect oneself against nsi and the wiles of enemies?

There was nothing like nsi, said the church, and even if there were, you only needed to pray to Chukwu and his saints and they would clear it all away. Obeying this injunction, Nnatu Ulili the tapster had before his baptism taken the ogwu in his house to the white fada. The priest had blessed him. Then all the ogwus that had been brought in that day had been piled before the church and burnt. But two days after Nnatu had made this religious gesture the enemy against whom he had made the ogwu had transformed himself into the fearful amosu bird, the drinker of blood, and had perched on Nnatu's roof and cried kwololom kwololom! with impunity. Nnatu had lain awake all through the night shivering and biting his finger-nails with regret. For if the ogwu had been there to protect him, the amosu wouldn't have dared come near his house. And if it did it would have dried up and so would have the body of the man whose soul inhabited the bird. The next morning Nnatu had run back to the dibia at Mbammili and made an even more powerful ogwu than the first. But this did not restore his peace of mind. For he had now offended Chukwu, God of the sky. Now he had loaded his soul with deadly sin and at his death Chukwu would throw him into the fire of the spirits.

The chief source of grievance however was the stiffness and lack of colour of the church. Spirit worship was a colourful drama with masquerading and fluting and singing and dancing. Furthermore the festivals were well spaced out through the year and integrated with the rhythms of the seasons. On these occasions relatives from the other villages visited their kindred, rejoiced with them and strengthened that bond of affection which bound them and sustained their lives.

The church on the other hand had no festivals. They had feasts of the saints referred to as 'unexpected Sunday' but one didn't feast then, one attended church and sang the monotonous church songs and came home again no more refreshed than if there had been nothing uncommon. There was 'kelesmes' too, if you could properly call that Christian. It seemed to have become more or less a day of rejoicing for everybody, Christians and spirit worshippers. And even at this period the church tried to curb the joy of its members. They forbade them to masquerade, for the masquerade, they said, was a pagan institution.

The new converts, faced with all these perplexities, usually drifted back to spirit worship which was a more satisfying experience with its awe taboos and appeal to piety. The steps the church leaders took to prevent this backsliding were prompt and downright. A militant group visited the house of the backslider and carried away his utensils and brought them into the church and kept them there until the owner redeemed them with a fine, and promised to be more diligent in future.

So when Danda showed signs of waning devotion he was brought up before the church court. His case was preceded by that of a farmer who came to demand his wife's mortar, taken away after his son had missed Sunday thrice.

'My wife cannot cook akpu without a mortar,' said the man. 'Must I starve . . .? Not to tell you a lie, people of our land there is nothing I value more than my belly.'

'The fine is a shilling,' said the catechist.

'Ahai!'

'Your son was fined for missing church. Were you not told that?'

'My son. But I am not my son—'

'You can make him behave. Take him by the ears and smack him soundly and he will become a better person.'

The farmer, intimidated, paid and walked away. But as soon as he got out of the premises he stopped some passers-by and told them of the alu the church had been committing.

The catechist wiped the streaming sweat from his face. He had had a hard morning.

'Well then, Danda,' he said smiling.

'Well then, Okoye Eze,' said Danda.

The catechist didn't like the name. But he said:

'Why did you not come to church last Sunday?'

'The Mbammili people invited me to a bring in and drink.'

'Is that an excuse you are not afraid to give?'

'If you don't like it I will give you another one. When Amumma Nmego's wife was alive he said to her: "Woman, if you don't like the truth, I will tell you a lie." '

There was laughter from the other members of the court. The catechist smiled.

'We have not come to laugh, Danda,' he said. 'Missing church is a deadly sin.'

'I know,' said Danda. 'But how could I miss a come and drink invitation from a great friend—'

Many others took turns to advise Danda. In the end he was fined sixpence.

'This thing is new,' said Danda to some friends.

'You still want to continue with them?' asked Nnoli Nwego.

'Let's look around first!'

The church made sure that he did continue by baptizing him at once. But before the ceremony his knowledge of the Catechism was tested. A large crowd turned up to see the event.

The first question was easy. Danda knew that God, Chukwu, is a spirit (muo) and that the same Chukwu made him. The next question was firewood-drier. Danda smiled, jingled his bells, looked at the ceiling but his memory was still dim. He turned to his teacher:

'Son of our fathers, do you know the thing?'

The teacher knew the thing but would not say it.

'You ought to know the answer,' said Father Royde, a young teacher interpreting. 'It is so simple.' He waited for a moment and then told Danda it.

'True.' laughed Danda. 'It is simple. Give us another one.' Father Royde smiled, infected by Danda's ebullience.

The next question puzzled Danda even more. The priest answered it also. The examination followed this pattern, the priest asking the questions and finding answers to them. In the end Danda was declared successful.

The crowd clapped their hands and cheered.

'Leave it to me,' said Danda acknowledging the applause.

The catechist then called for the church Register.

'What name would Danda want to be baptized with?' The crowd surged nearer to hear what Danda would say. Great importance was attached to the baptismal name. It had as it were come to replace the old titular praise name.

'What name would I use,' said Danda. 'It is hard to know. Some people call me Danda, others Rain.'

'This is different,' said the catechist. 'You must take an oibo name or the name of a saint.'

'You are talking,' said Danda glancing expressively at the people around.

'Take Peter, Danda,' one of them said.

'Take Michael.'

'Don't listen to them. Take John.'

'Quiet, everybody,' said the catechist. 'Now then, Danda, what is it going to be?'

'Michael then or Peter . . . anything. It is nothing to break heads over.'

'You must think hard. Don't just say anything.'

'Write down whatever you like.'

'I will choose for him,' the catechist told Father Royde. 'Danda, you will be Robinson.'

This choice was loudly applauded.

'Robinson Araba,' the catechist recorded the name.

'Ahai,' laughed Danda. 'It is sweet in the mouth. But will my mother know how to call it?'

The next point: how old was Danda. In what year was he born? 'What a question,' said Danda. 'Listen to that, people of our land. In what year was I born? How should I know? Was I present on the day I was conceived?'

'He does not know,' said the catechist. 'But I can guess. He would be about thirty.'

The baptism was to take place two days later. On that day, Danda was told, he was to come to church with his father.

'Your talk is good. Yes, I will bring my father but you must stay behind me.' Danda cowered and ran a few paces forward in mock fear. 'Yes, I will bring my father, if he will come.'

CHAPTER NINE

Very early that morning the cry of women went up to the heavens. The Uwadiegwus were mourning Mgbafo Ezira. The women stood before the doors of their gates, cupped their mouths and wailed that what men had done to Mgbafo Ezira was not good. After that they went back home, dotted their faces with white clay, came out again and walked round Aniocha killing evil spirits on their way.

As soon as it was full dawn the ceremony began. The fat cow was led to the shrine. The men came after it and when they reached the grounds they spread goats' skins and sat down. The priest began intoning the prayers.

'God of the sky who created the world—'

The shrine is wrapped by a forest of thick gnarled trees so that even after the harmattan sun has come up, biting, it is still cool, very quiet. There is a feeling of expectancy. Some paces farther away a small stream named after the god gurgled as it flowed down its narrow valley to Mbammili. The earthen god squatted with its legs curled and stared at the worshippers with its cowrie eyes.

'Great father receive your offering.

The suns are gone away and the rains will come.

Give us good planting.'

The other worshippers formed a semicircle round the priest. Nwokeke, subtly distinguished from the others, sat on a decorated stool. Araba, Idengeli and other ozos asserted themselves nearby. Okelekwu carried his whip on his shoulder. Nwafo Ugo's face had on an expression of comic gravity.

'Spirits of our fathers, come and eat oji.

Bad spirits come and eat oji and be ashamed.'

The priest splashed more wine at the foot of the statue.

'Let the spirits of those who killed Mgbafo Ezira carry the alu. And let us be free from blame—'

He called for the cow. Two young men untied it from a tree and dragged it resisting to the god.

The Uwadiegwus relaxed and began to rummage in their cowskin bags for snuff and cola . . .

Not far away the Christians prepared for Baptism. All the candidates carried lighted candles and stood around the altar. The catechist waddled into the church and looked them over.

'Where is Danda?' he asked.

'He has not come.'

'Oh!' The catechist walked round examining the certificates of the candidates. There were old men, old women as well as babies.

The catechist counted the latter . . .

'Only eight,' he said.

'There are more to come,' said a woman. 'Those who are gone to call them have not returned.'

There were two Christian missions in Aniocha. And there was keen rivalry between them in the gathering of new members. Each party usually concentrated on the babies. They would take them from their mothers, sometimes by promising to educate them free, and baptize them, and in that way ensure that they belonged to their own group.

Father Royde arrived, dressed in his cassock and surplice, his velvet stole trailing from the back of his neck over his shoulders down to the knees. Like the catechist he looked the catechumen over and remarked the absence of Danda.

'Who are his sponsors?'

'I don't know,' said the catechist. 'I have not seen Danda since the examination day.'

'We shall wait a little while.' The priest began checking the equipment for baptism: holy water and oil, cotton wool. The incense was already burning in the censer.

They waited. After some time two men came into the church followed by many mothers carrying their babies.

'How many?' asked the catechist.

'Six,' said one of the church leaders.

'You have done well.'

Danda still hadn't come. So they had to perform the ceremony without him. At the end, as the catechumen were dispersing the priest called the catechist and asked:

'Is that man's home far? The singer's?'

'A little far.'

'We are going to see him.'

The catechist rubbed his bald head doubtfully but said nothing. The priest took off his surplice and stole and gave them to a young mass-server. Then only in his cassock he followed the catechist.

In the compound of Araba they found nobody but a little girl who was playing a game with an imaginary opponent, at whom she was now shouting.

'You won't cheat me.'

She stopped as the men came in and stared at them with big eyes. 'Where is Danda?' the catechist asked her.

'Danda? He has gone to the church. They are giving him the water of God there, and he has a new name.'

'When did he go?'

'It is long . . . Wait, let me remember. Yes, it is long.'

The catechist explained to the priest.

'I wonder where he could have gone to?' Then he asked, pointing to the girl: 'Does she come to church?'

'Do you come to church, Ada?' asked the catechist. 'I have received the water of God,' she said. 'My name is Teresa.'

'That's right, stay well.'

'Stay well.' She followed them and from a safe distance watched them until they were out of sight.

At a point in the road the catechist suddenly stopped and listened. 'There is music somewhere. And he may be there.'

'Our man?'

'Danda . . . These people have a festival of some sort.'

'Let's go and see.'

They struck a narrow bush path which after a while went into a thickly festooned wood. The ground here was thickly carpeted with rotten leaves. The place had a curious aloofness. But suddenly it seemed as if the huge old trees had become aware of the visitors for they suddenly began to whisper to one another. This went on for a spell before they resumed their phlegmatic dignity.

'They worship these,' said Father Royde, pointing to the white sheets which draped some of the trees and the sacrificial offerings left at their feet.

'They do,' agreed the catechist.

They were approaching the shrine for the deep silence was ruffled every now and then by the chirrup of the oja. A few minutes more and the forest came to an end and the two men stumbled into music.

The cow had been slaughtered and the errant spirit of the wronged woman laid. Cola and baked cassava had been served. Now the flute was calling the great men of the

umunna and at each call somebody answered 'Oi! oi! oi!
I am here.'

The chieftain was the first to sight the white man who
had stopped before the clearing and seemed to be hesitating.

'Ask the white man what he wants, Nwobu.'

Nwobu shambled forward to the visitors. After a while
he returned and whispered to the chieftain.

'Danda,' said Nwokeke, 'your people want you.'

Danda had just fluted the praise name of Okelekwu when
he heard his name called. He turned and said:

'Eh?'

'Look over there and see your friends.'

Danda looked and saw. He jingled up to them.

'Have you finished the water of God?' he asked.

'Why were you not in the church?'

'I was coming there but stopped to take some palm
wine.'

'So you were drinking with spirit-worshippers!'

'What is wrong with that?'

'Don't you know it is a deadly sin?'

'Ahai,' said Danda scratching his head, 'deadly sin?
Your word is bent, stretch it.'

The catechist was going to say something more but the
priest stopped him and said: 'Tell him to come with us.'

'He says there will be serious punishment for you if you
do not come with us.'

'I will come . . . Go ahead and wait for me in the church.'

'Now, you son of a beast.'

'This is strange,' said Danda. 'Has agwu risen into your
head? Do you think I am a child?'

The catechist fumed.

'Stuttering,' said Danda. And he turned his back to them
and jingled to the umunna.

'What did they say to you, Danda?' asked Nwafo Ugo.

'Ahai,' said Danda. 'Some people say that Danda is a
tortoise, others that he is mad. I am not mad, people of our
land, but I am not sure that I am sane. Give us palm wine.'

The church had the last word in this affair. Two market
weeks later they came to Araba's compound. There were

63

four strong men and two women. They surrounded the obi.

'What is it?' asked Araba eyeing them coldly.

'We want Danda's things,' they said.

'Why do you come to me? That is Danda's hut over there.'

The Christians hesitated but finally, overawed by Araba's controlled force, they turned and walked up to the small hut near the gate. A few minutes later they returned holding aloft a disreputable-looking sleeping mat. This was the only thing that Danda possessed.

CHAPTER TEN

The scorch season was dying. The happiest time of the year, the season for feasts, when men and women laughed with all their teeth and little boys, their mouths oily oily, ran about the lanes blowing the crops of chicken to make balloons. In a few days the rain season would come and bring with it a ceaseless round of labour. And men would leave their homes with the first cry of the cock and would not return until the chicken came back to roost. Already the bushes were on fire and the acrid smell of burning permeated the earth.

Over the flames hovered the kite mourning the death of the year. In a few days he would flee the land to better places to escape the rain. But some people say that it is not the death of the scorch season that the kite mourns but the death of his mother. They tell how one day he culled pumpkin leaves from his farm and gave them to his mother to cook. But he hadn't known that pumpkin leaves shrink after they have been cooked. When his mother served him it, he was amazed by its smallness and in a fit of rage killed her. Then panicking he took the dead body and threw it into the flames of a bush fire. At the end of each scorch season, especially when he was hungry, he would remember his mother and go looking for her in the flames crying:

'Nnemu-o oku gbagbulu-u-u!'

Danda too did not look forward with eagerness to the coming of the rain season. But that night the moon was out and the night was fine. He determined to enjoy what remained of the season of the sun. So taking up his flute, he chirruped his favourite tunes up and down Aniocha.

The people in the surrounding villages had also come out to bid farewell to one half of the year. From Eziakpaka up the hill the warrior song trickled down as if from the sky. But before it reached Aniocha it had to filter through the huge forest at the boundary and eventually arrived from the bowels of the earth.

'Iye-e-e, eiye eye!'

Everywhere Danda went there were exciting scenes. Women left their pots of bitter-leaf soup on the fire and stood tip-toe overlooking the outer walls of their compound. Children climbed ladders or orange trees and looked out. Dogs followed them and barked. The women called out:

'Rain, is there anything passing?'

'My wives, cook the bitter-leaf soup properly. I am coming right in.'

'That's it.' They clapped and cheered.

Danda fluted on. When he came to the compound of a man he was intimate with he called out that man's praise name. The responses of the men, depending on each person's character, were varied. Some remained in their obi and roared 'I hear.' Others burst out and looked over their walls and cried 'ewe ewe ewe!'

Danda came to the church premises and stood watching the tall ogbu trees. They had spread their arms and were rising up to the heavens. The moon too was coming down to meet them. Somewhere between the earth and the sky both met.

Danda fluted on inventing many variations to some well-known themes . . .

The Uwadiegwu umunna had gathered at the ogwe, a wooden stand rising in tiers, consisting of wooden benches placed on forked stakes. The men sat on the benches and snuffed. The women had formed a circle in an open square adjacent to the stands and were singing and clapping vigorously. A girl stood in the middle dancing the warrior dance and cutting through the air with the right hand in imitation of the slash of the matchet.

> 'Obulu nimalu aja.
> Gbuo nu mma ndi Agbaja
> Iye-e-e eiye eye.'

There was some colourful quality in the refrain which dispelled the spirit of darkness. For the night, even with the moon shining, has a heavy pressure that subdues the heart. But the song made the heart light and the eyes shine.

> 'Iye-e-e eiye eye
> Gbuo nu ma ndi Agbaja
> Iye—'

The song was interrupted by the entry of Danda. There was a roar of greeting.

'Rain! Is he drunk?'

'Daughters of beauty!' shouted Danda. 'All the men love you. If there is any man who doesn't love you let him put his head in the fire and see how he likes it. That song again, hoa!' And accompanied by his oja the girls began the song of the Anambala canoemen. The dancer this time was Ekeama Idemmili the youngest wife of the chieftain. Laughing merrily, she flounced up and down. Her hands holding an imaginary paddle made the rhythmic motions of ploughing through the bubbling stream.

> 'Ugbom ana-a-a
> Anambala
> O na-a
> Anambala.'

The men at the ogwe looked on, rapt in admiration.

'She is bright,' said a tapster.

'Bright, that's the word,' agreed Nwafo Ugo. 'I wonder from which village Nwokeke brought her. She is different from the women of these parts.'

'That was what I thought when first I saw her. I said to myself: this woman is not one of us.'

'No,' said Okelekwu waving his whip. 'She is from Umukrushe.'

'From where?'

'Umukrushe.'

There was a burst of laughter.

'Okelekwu, my brother, what did you say it was? People of our land wait a moment. Let the name reach the depths of my ear.'

'Umukrushe.'

'Ahai! The names that exist in this world!'

'But does it exist?' said the herdsman. 'Or is it just like a story?'

'It exists,' said Okelekwu, 'I have been there.' There was respectful silence. Okelekwu was a traveller. 'Yes,' he continued, 'when first I saw Ekeama I said to myself: "She is from Umukrushe." Then I asked Nwokeke and he said to me: "You are right." They have queer ways, those people. For instance the men do not pay bride price. Nwokeke paid nothing for Ekeama.'

'Then I will go there,' said Nwafo Ugo. 'What have I been waiting for? How long does it take to reach the place, Okelekwu?'

'Three days. You go in the land-boat.'

'Count me out,' said Nwafo. 'If I have to stay in a land-boat for three days I will be taken out in pieces.'

'But what I cannot understand is why they call themselves Umuku . . .'

'Umukrushe.'

'Call it whatever name you like. No village has the right to give itself such a name.'

'No,' said Nwafo, 'what interests me is that the people do not ask for bride price.'

'It is strange now that you should return to that point, Nwafo,' laughed the herdsman. 'Tell us the truth. What is wrong with your wife, Nwuka?'

'Yes, tell us!' roared the others. 'There is something inside your voice.'

'Well, every man wants to have one more wife if he can,' said Nwafo a little lamely. 'How many of you would not like to fill your obi?'

'No,' said the herdsman. 'Who, with his eyes open, would want to cover himself with burning coals?'

The others laughed, some uneasily.

The singers had changed back to the warrior dance. Ekeama was at the moment demonstrating how the Agbaja warriors shot the arrow.

> 'Obulu ni mala Aja
> Gbaa nu uta ndi Agbaja
> Iy-e-e eiye eiye
> Gbuo nu mma ndi Agbaja—'

'You know what happened yesterday?' said Nwafo.

'What happened?' asked the herdsman smiling ironically.

'We were kneading mud for the new building of Okafo Nwalo. Then Ekeama dancing about and laughing and not looking which way she was going fell into the mud pit. She was not hurt but she could not climb out, the pit was deep. Danda was with us too—have I told you?—not in the pit but playing his oja outside. Then he saw the girl fall in. He stopped, leaned over the pit and lifted her up. But this is the one that will interest you—he did not let her down.'

'How do you mean?'

'She clung tightly to him, enclosed his head with her hands and pressed her face to his. With that hold he walked with her round the pit, and we laughed. Well, when he put her down do you know what she said? Ask me what she said. She said: 'I do better than that in private." '

'Great woman,' said the herdsman.

The other men watched more attentively. Where Danda had succeeded they themselves shouldn't expect to fail.

'It is their way,' said Okelekwu. 'The women of her land

are free. They are not stable. If you marry one of them today she may run off with another tomorrow.'

'Will her father return my bride price?'

'They have no bride price. I have just said so.'

'That's it. You see what happens when there is no bride price. So, Nwafo, do not go to your place, Umukulu—what's the horrid name again—to marry.'

'I will.'

'Go ahead. You will eat pepper.'

The night had gone far now, the moon itself looked weary and the air was becoming damp. The dancers had stopped and were dispersing. The men, too, rose and went. The ogwe was empty save for two people: Danda and Ekeama who for long afterwards whispered and made love under the cover of an ogbu tree.

CHAPTER ELEVEN

'Let me ask you, does day reach your hut or not? How long do you want to sleep? Are you a white man?'

Danda heard only dimly these questions fired at him with such rapidity. He stirred drowsily, yawned and said 'eh?'

'What is "eh"? Is today a feast day?' Araba sniffed angrily and went back to his obi.

Danda yawned again and slowly slid his right leg down the raised mud which served him as a bed. Then mentally he dared the other leg to follow. This limb declined to. The first leg hesitated, gave in and returned to its partner. Danda cradled his head more comfortably with his cloak and sighed cosily. It had rained the previous night and the morning was cool and leaden. Danda went back to sleep.

He was aroused again by angry bellows which seemed to be proceeding from the obi. After a smell of regret he rose, wrapped himself closely with the cloak and set out.

Araba was tapping his leg impatiently on the ground. At

last he cried out: 'What has happened to the woman. Chinwe!'

'Ee!' a muffled voice came from one of the outhouses. 'Bring the food, quick.'

A tall light-complexioned woman strode into the obi. She carried two large plates, one of akpu and the other of egusi soup.

'Why did it take so long?' Araba asked.

'I was busy with other things. The whole burden of this compound is on my shoulders . . .' Her tone was rising steadily but when she looked at Araba and saw how calm he was she lowered it. 'I suppose I am your carrying pad,' she concluded suddenly.

She was the fifth or was it the sixth wife. Araba couldn't remember the order. He did not often see many of his ten wives. But no one could help seeing Chinwe with her hand-some figure and fine eyes which were always flashing out either in anger or in joy. Araba had for some time recognized her as a favourite. He ate her cooking most frequently and often asked her to represent him in some of his money affairs. She liked the privilege but thought it politic to complain about it.

'You will go to Obunagu today,' Araba said to her as she was turning back, 'and collect the money your uncle owes me.'

'I am very busy today,' she said. 'I will go tomorrow.'

'You will go today.'

'It is well,' she said noncommittally and walked off smiling to herself.

Araba was the first to rise from the food. He scraped his fingers with a short knife, wiped off the remaining splotches of food on his wrapper, and waited impatiently for Danda. Danda soon was ready.

'You won't need the cloak, I think,' said Araba.

'True word,' Danda rose and jingled to his hut. Araba went into the barn to collect the yams.

Danda stood in his hut thinking. For the first time he saw what a disadvantage the bells on his cloak could be. But Araba must have been deeply engrossed with his yam for he did not heed the jingles.

At last he came out, carrying a long shallow basket loaded with yams. 'Danda!' he called. 'What is it now?'

There was no answer. Araba walked up to the small hut and peeped inside. There was nobody there.

'Danda!' he called again.

'Danda is not in,' said one of the wives who had just returned from the stream. 'He must be in Eziakpaka by now.'

'What do you mean?'

'I saw him just now crossing the woods over there.'

'He will eat pepper,' said Araba furiously. And he went and carried the long basket and stumped out and away.

He returned later just as the night was covering the earth and for a long time sat in the obi snuffing, very pleased with his day's work. He had hoed the whole field which he had thought would require the combined energies of both him and Danda.

Just then a small boy of about eleven came into the compound and Araba recognized him as the son of Okelekwu.

'A letter came,' he said after greeting Araba.

'True word?'

The boy dipped in his pocket and brought it out and gave it to him.

Araba turned the letter around and then said as if he could read it: 'It is from Onuma.'

'It is,' said the boy.

'Take a seat, son. And let's hear what it says. No, wait a moment, let's call the woman. Mgbeke!'

A thick reedy voice replied from one of the outhouses. As they waited Araba told the boy of Onuma. He liked little boys and always spoke to them as to equals.

'How many years is it now since the white man's war ended, son?'

'Four years,' said the boy. 'It ended in 1945. It is now 1949.'

'Then Onuma has been out eight years. I remember he went off four years before the war ended. And since then he has never seen this land. That is as it should be. What

71

does a man have to come to this our land for? We toil and feed on sand. But those who go out to the towns can fill their bellies properly ... They didn't take him to the wars and we are thankful to the spirits that own this compound for that ... I saw Idengeli's son when he returned from the wars and he looked like an old man. Their skins toughen in the wars ...'

After a few more minutes he said: 'Hai! What is keeping her ...?' Then, turning to the boy, he said: 'Do you see, son? Women are like fire coals which a man open-eyed heaps on his head!'

But there was certainly nothing fiery about Mgbeke as she sat on a stool and carefully turned her back on her husband. She was very timid. There was a time when Araba shouted at her. He usually bullied his women. But Mgbeke had shrunk so much from violence that he had had to leave her alone. She had curled more and more into herself so that neighbours often doubted whether she still lived. She seldom came out during the day. If she wanted to fetch water from the common stream or to buy salt from a neighbour she did so in the night, gliding noiselessly like a ghost. But with Araba she had a claim to recognition, being the mother of the most promising of his sons.

'Our man has written,' he said and tossed the letter to her.

She darted at it, picked it up and pressed it to her bosom. 'Such a long time,' she murmured and laughed hysterically.

'What did he say?' she picked up courage to ask.

'Wait, you will hear.'

'I will wait.'

The boy pierced open the letter and read it through and interpreted slowly. The facts were drunk in thirstily by his hearers. Onuma had written to say that he would shortly be coming home. His parents were to find him a wife. And he had sent money for the purpose.

'The letter was well written,' said Araba in a knowing voice. 'But where is the money?'

The boy extracted a postal order from the envelope and explained its mysteries.

Araba took the slip, pored over it and remarked:

'The white man is clever. A small piece of paper is equal to thirty pounds. Wives cost more of course but it is a beginning.'

'He sent me money, too,' the woman whispered to the boy. Araba turned sharply and said 'Eh?'

The woman curled up, clutching firmly the postal order the boy had slipped to her.

'What's that boy?' said Araba.

'Nothing,' said the boy. He would not inform.

Araba looked from one to the other then shrugged his shoulders and began to snuff.

Mgbeke whispered to the boy and drew him away to her hut to read the letter all over again for her.

Araba watched them go and decided that when Onuma returned he would speak to him. The proper thing to do was to send money to him, Araba, and then leave him to decide whether it would be proper to give it to any of his wives . . .

He had just finished night food when the boy came out of the women's wing and started home. Araba called him into the obi and in a conspiratorial whisper asked:

'How much money did he send her?'

'Money?' said the boy, stalling.

'Never mind,' said Araba. 'I know . . . Have you eaten food?'

'Yes.'

'Good.' Araba thought for a minute then asked: 'You say he asked for a girl who has been to school?'

'That's what the letter says.'

'The money is not big enough. Girls who have been to school cost money. But if he wants a girl who has been to school we will get her for him . . . He will have to work harder and make more money that is all. And I want something for myself too. I am to entertain the ozo this year . . . But everything will be well . . . all will be well . . .'

The boy rose to go.

'You will not fear the night, son?' asked Araba.

'No.'

73

'That's it. I will give you a leg to the gate.' And Araba led him to the gate and stood there watching him go, presenting as it were his body as an assurance against fear.

When he returned to the obi he had taken a firm decision and he called Nwamma to announce it to her. She came and sat down beside the palm fruit light and Araba noting with satisfaction her calm, smooth manner and wise eyes knew that she would understand. Nwamma was the first wife and perhaps because she had been with him longest and perhaps because both of them had worn off the friction which would always exist between man and wife, she was the only person with whom he was at ease. He complained to her of the behaviour of the other wives and was glad of her support in many of his quarrels.

'I was to go to the farm this morning with Danda,' he said. 'But after morning food he disappeared.'

'Oh.'

'Is that all you have to say? Is that all—' Araba was raising his voice but stopped in time.

'What else can I say?' she said.

'When they look for me and fail to see me he will be the one to take my obi?'

'Yes.'

'Well, he won't be. I will leave everything to Onuma.'

'Do whatever you think fit,' she said. 'I won't take Danda's side. This afternoon when he came home I warned him. I said, "Danda, you cannot let your father do all the work while you flute about." Yes, I spoke strongly to him.'

'He came home today?'

'He came to eat afternoon food.'

'That's it. You feed him too much . . . And I am going to stop it . . . I will not see him in my obi again. I have thrown him out.'

'That is too much—'

'He will go about like the akologholi he is. Then he will understand that food does not fall down from the birds. Yes . . . hunger will tell him what I have never succeeded in telling him. Ahai! . . . And see here, if I hear that you feed him either in here or outside it will be a cause for quarrel

74

between you and me.'

Nwamma nodded.

'It is well . . .'

She went.

Everything will be well . . . The hand of the spirits seemed to be in it all . . . What happiness! The very day one son lost his place in the obi, another proved worthy of it . . . Araba had often tried to disinherit Danda but had always been faced with this difficulty that there might be nobody else with whom to replace him. Now everything had worked out well. All will be well. Araba had a sense of extreme well-being, his body and mind were relaxed, the body from a good day's work and the mind from having taken a firm decision.

In that mellow mood he remembered that he hadn't touched his day's calabash of wine . . . He wouldn't be able to finish it; he would have to send for Okelekwu to drink with him. He rose briskly and walked over to the corner of the room where the calabash stood. He held it by the neck and raised it up. It came away with suspicious ease. He laid it down again and it rolled blithely away. The calabash was empty.

CHAPTER TWELVE

'This compound is large,' said Nwokeke.

'True word,' agreed Nwobu Esili.

'Yes,' said Araba. 'Udeji spread himself when he built it.'

'It is large,' repeated Nwokeke unslinging his cowskin bag and laying it on his knees.

Araba was alert. The visit had taken him by surprise. Since the day the matter of the chieftaincy was decided he had not been on visiting terms with Nwokeke.

'How are my wives?' said Nwokeke.

'They are all well,' said Araba absentmindedly . . . After a brief, pregnant pause he said: 'I will give you cola.'

'You have done well.'

Araba looked into a beautiful trough carved into the form of a bird, took a cola from inside it and gave it to Nwokeke.

'No, son of our fathers,' said the chieftain. 'It is your due.' Araba prayed over the cola and broke it. There were four blades.

'Good luck!' roared Nwokeke. 'Brother, there will be many in your obi.'

'Good luck to everybody,' said Araba giving two blades to his visitors.

Nwobu dipped his in the ose oji inside the trough, and ate it. Nwokeke regarded his own for some time and when he thought nobody was looking slipped it into his bag. Araba, who had observed the movement, frowned.

'Yes,' said Nwokeke, 'there is a fine Ikenga too. Who worked it?'

'I cannot remember,' said Araba.

Some moments passed in uneasy silence. Then Nwokeke, clearing his throat, began his story. He told it evenly without heat but after he had finished Araba's heart was on fire. But his tone as he spoke was firm.

'You saw him with her?'

'No, but somebody did.'

'That man may have been telling a lie?'

'Not him. Besides, Ekeama has confessed. Danda I have not been able to see. They tell me he has fled to Eziakpaka.'

'And what will you do?'

'Do? It is hard . . . This age doesn't permit violence or I would have had it out with him. There is only one thing to do, take the case to the umunna.'

Araba couldn't hide his satisfaction. If the matter were hushed up in the family his reputation in Aniocha would remain intact.

'It is well,' said Araba. 'When I see Danda I will ask him . . . When do you call the umunna?'

'The umunna . . . ah yes . . . But can't you see, son of our fathers. The matter is more serious than that.' Nwokeke waved his hand in a helpless manner. 'It has gone beyond the umunna. The ozo, too, must be told. You know our rules.'

Araba knew the rules. He himself had severely denounced a man who had committed the same offence only a few months before. In the olden days adulterers were killed outright. Now, however, the punishment was different but for a man of honour no less mortifying. The parties were first fined then dressed in rags, broken bottles, and bags of white ants, and walked round the village to receive the taunts of the populace. If Danda underwent such an experience it would be a long time before Araba could look the Aniocha people in the face.

'It is not a small thing,' resumed Nwokeke. 'We must see it through to the end. I don't like it but the whole of Aniocha must know about it . . .'

Araba had been thinking hard. And immediately Nwokeke finished speaking some hard decision formed in his eyes.

'Is that everything?' he asked.

'Everything,' said Nwokeke surprised.

'It is well.'

'So then we have to go?' He rose smiling and slung his cowskin bag across his shoulder. 'I greet you.'

Nwobu followed him out. . . .

For a long time Araba watched the small pool of light which the dying sun shed in the western part of the obi . . . It was receding little by little and finally disappeared altogether. In the bushes nearby birds of various species were making their homing calls.

Tum tum Kpalakwukwu! Tum tum Kpalakwukwu! That was kpalakwukwu the pigeon.

The chickens too were rushing home. One mother hen led her chicks to her home under the ogbu tree dedicated to one of the compound gods. There were eight chicks altogether. Six crept under their mother's wings. The other two were playfully climbing on to her back and falling each time. The mother hen clucked happily: Kwom! kwom! kwom!

Outside the compound the tall palms had begun to do their evening exercise nodding and stretching preparatory to turning in. The night arrived with great suddenness. And the moon which was in its half-way stage came with it.

Araba was in need of somebody to talk to. And happily just at this moment Nwamma brought him his night food of akpu and bitter-leaf soup. As he fed she talked and he listened and now and then threw in a sympathetic remark.

'The hungry days must be very near. Everybody in Aniocha is mad. There is that man of the Uruoji umunna, the one who has a squint. He was caught carrying somebody's palm mats. But when he appeared before the umunna he denied it. He said the man who caught him was lying. And they took him before the Alusi and do you know, he swallowed those oaths, pia! as if they were water. I have never heard of such foolhardiness.'

'Agwu,' said Araba laconically. 'It has always been strong in their family.'

'And Chinwe nearly fought today with the wife of Idengeli. We were sowing corn and there was a dispute over a single mound. Idengeli's wife said it was inside their own strip and we said no . . .'

Araba made no comment. A man shouldn't engage in such women's quarrels.

'I am going down to Mbammili early tomorrow . . . Ada has a swollen arm.' Ada was her daughter married into Mbammili.

'Has the ocimbo blooded her?'

'No.'

'I have some ogwu that you can take to her.'

'Yes . . .' Nwamma hesitated. 'Yes . . . I haven't seen Danda since yesterday . . .'

'Nwokeke is looking for him too . . . And when . . .' He didn't go further. Bells jingled, the door of the gate banged open and a voice was heard bawling.

'Father of ours, is there palm wine in your house?'

'You will drink the palm wine in the land of the spirits,' roared Araba springing out. A moment later he came back trailing a short, wicked matchet.

'Have you killed him?' Nwamma asked.

Araba said nothing and crept into the obi and resumed his food.

'Have you killed him?'

The lump of akpu which was moving slowly to his mouth stopped half-way and Araba said:

'I told you to warn the akalogholi off my compound, didn't I?'

It was now Nwamma's turn to keep silent. She walked calmly to the gate and out. There she searched everywhere, through the clump of pineapple bush at the side of the outer walls; in the small copse adjoining the road, but there was no body. She was wondering what to do next when from the darkness bells jingled in unison up to her.

'Sh!' she said to them.

'What's the trouble, Mother?' said Danda's voice.

'What have you done?'

'You mean why I drank . . .?'

'You have done something bad, bad.'

'No. I have never done anything bad.'

'You mustn't come into the obi tonight. Don't come tomorrow. Come only when his anger has gone down . . .'

'Ahai . . . I won't come back until he sends for me.'

'Eh?'

'If I go I won't return until he sends for me.'

'I know nothing,' said Nwamma shrugging her shoulders and going back home.

Danda merged once more into the darkness. Some minutes later his oja was heard ruffling the silence of the night. A few people who lived close to the main road left their houses and tried to see who the musician was.

CHAPTER THIRTEEN

Araba's son was back home. The news formed the chief fare of local gossip for some days. Relatives from the surrounding towns came to the obi, rejoiced with the family, prayed for the newcomer and went home again. Then it was the turn of the umunna. Each of them had had a cup and as usual declared a moral on it.

'Yes, I must tell you the truth, son,' said Idengeli. 'The man who makes money makes it not for himself alone, but for the umunna . . . If the road proves good it becomes the property of all . . . Some men I know make money and give none of it to their people. That type of money is useless. It is like food which one eats alone, never sweet.'

'True word,' agreed Akumma Nwego, stretching his hand for a cup of wine.

The calabash was empty and Onuma filled it again from a huge pot at one corner of the room. He was a younger copy of his father, short, with the same disproportionately large head but lacking the ferocity of expression.

'Welcome again, son,' said Okelekwu. 'Uwadiegwu will have its share of the white man's good things. You are our share.'

'He is our share,' said Nwafo Ugo, belching.

Araba said nothing, merely snuffed and listened. His heart was full. Often he would gaze fixedly at his son and then from him to the bright things that had been bought in the city. Onuma occupied Danda's hut, but Araba had ordered that his things be brought to the obi to be presented to the family gods. A new bicycle as sparkling as they made them stood by the old ikenga. Finely worked glasses received the protection of the ofo. But the instrument to which most attention was paid was an iron box which talked and sang.

'I saw one like that in Ikolo umunna some days ago,' said Nwafo Ugo. 'It is the work of a magician. The white man has eaten the amosu. He makes a box talk, men of our lands. Hai!'

'Let's hear it.'

Onuma, smiling, played an American crooner on the gramophone. The men listened for a few moments then looked at each other dismayed. What they had just heard did not sound right. Nwafo Ugo was especially sceptic. A drummer himself, he had a keen ear for what properly constituted harmony.

'What do you call this, son of ours?' he asked, making a face. 'Is it music or what?'

'It is oibo music. You don't like it?'

'Who would?'

Onuma removed the disc and substituted for it a recording of an Ibo song and in a few moments the vigorous notes of the ogwulugwu cracked out. The faces of the men cleared, their eyes brightened, they moved their limbs in time with the music.

'Ahai!' cried Nwafo. 'There is no doubt about this at all. This is music (egwu).'

The boisterous sounds cracked and vibrated through the Obi. And soon the salty harsh voice of the vocalist began to dominate the instruments.

'It is Okoye Udeozo's voice,' roared Nwafo excitedly. 'One of the great voices of our time.'

'He is dead now.'

'How he used to draw people. Hai!'

'Have I told you,' said Okelekwu moved out of his habitual phlegm, 'one day I was on a journey and came into Ubom, that place where men drink palm wine and women farm— they are a lazy people. I reached there in the night, and my legs were heavy—heavy. I had walked twenty miles that day. But when they told me that Okoye Udeozo was singing at Agbenu five miles away my tiredness left me. Just like that, sacham!' Okelekwu snapped his fingers. 'With many other men of the place I set out by the moonlight to Agbenu. Okoye Udeozo was there, men of our lands. And after I had heard him my stomach was filled. That voice! He is dead now,' Okelekwu ended in his usual mournful manner.

'Everybody whose name is known is dead,' said Nwafo. 'The world is spoilt.'

On this note they took their leave.

'I shall come back tomorrow, son,' said Nwafo. 'And on other days too. You will make more money. The eyes of your grandfather, and they were fire eyes too, are open. And we will come again and drink. I won't miss my turn.'

'No,' said Akumma Nwego pulling softly at his charred pipe. They went. All but an old man who sat rubbing his white beard glancing uneasily at Onuma. At last he mumbled: 'Our son, did you see my boy?'

'Yes.'

A little spark appeared in the old man's beady eyes.

'Is he well?'

'Yes, very well.'

'That's it,' said the old man rising painfully. 'We can only hope in the one who lives in the sky . . .' Just before he passed out of the obi he turned back and asked: 'He didn't tell you when he was coming back?'

'He said soon.'

'It is well . . . Let him stay up there and fill himself . . . All will be well. All will be well . . .' And muttering feebly he went.

'Who is his son?' Onuma asked Araba.

He told him.

The boy had been out of the town for some ten years. Rumour had it that he had been lucky, obtained an important Government job and bought a car. He had since given no thought to his father. The old man's hut had been threatening to fall for two years, but each time the umunna had propped it up. Finally they had decided to send some young men to the town to speak to the old man's son. But the messengers hadn't seen him for he was said to have gone to another place.

'Does anybody know where he is, now?'

'No.'

But each time somebody returned from abroad the old man would ask him: 'Did you see my son?' To him all places outside the ten towns were the same.

They had now all gone and Araba was free to talk with Onuma. He had looked forward to this opportunity. But now that it was before him he didn't know what to say . . . Should he tell him of his quarrels and enlist his support? But when Araba looked at him and saw Onuma's bored expression he doubted if he would be a warm enough partisan . . .

'They made Nwokeke chief . . . Did you know?'

'They told me.'

'And he has fought me since then but has found me strong. He wants our ozala but he won't get it . . .'

There was another pause.

Finally Araba said: 'I am not happy with my children. Danda is an akalogholi, the other one neither the spirits nor men know where he is. You have never heard of him?'

'Of him?'

'Were you listening?'

'O yes . . . who?'

'Where is Nwibe?'

'The last time I heard of him he was beyond the frontier. He had escaped into the French territories. They tell me that there he is a boxer. He fights other people for money.'

'They will kill him,' said Araba vindictively . . . 'And perhaps it is just as well. Since he went away he has never written. But all will be well.'

Onuma was weary. Since the previous day when he returned he had been up entertaining and never had a rest. Araba, observing the fatigue, remarked:

'Let it be till tomorrow.'

Onuma rose at once and walked to Danda's hut. But in spite of his tiredness he spent some time pondering about what the peasant had said: 'You will make money and we will come again and drink.' If he continued providing as much palm wine as he had been giving for two days, in a short time he would be penniless.

CHAPTER FOURTEEN

The hut stood alone, only backed by a number of akpaka trees. It had once belonged to a queer family with the name of Ndulu who for some reason or the other had abjured the society of their kind and gone to live in the wilds. The man had died some years later. But the wife had stuck to their home. After a year the Aniocha men had frightened her back to society with terrible-looking masquerades.

'She was a wild animal when she came to live with us,' said Nnoli Nwego spreading his huge bulk on the raised

mud in the small porch adjoining the living room. 'I saw
her one evening and said to her: "Greetings, woman." And
you know what she said to me? She said: "Do you think I
am mad?" "No," I said, "you are not mad, you are as bright
as ripe palm nuts." "No more of that, no more of that,"
she said.'

'True word,' said Okoli Mbe and tried to adjust his
bottom more comfortably to the short walking-stick on the
head of which he balanced himself. He was a short man
with a narrow head and sharp, cunning eyes. People said
that his name, Mbe (Tortoise), was most appropriate. Just
as the tortoise was always the centre of all fables so Okoli
Mbe knew of all alus that were perpetrated in Aniocha. 'I
used to greet her as I greeted other women. "Greetings,
my wife." But she would turn back fiercely: "I am not
your wife." '

The hut was built on the top of an incline. From its back
one saw a wooden valley which was now bathed with
lazy sunlight. A thin road climbed the slope and led by
stunted bushes to the village. Women were now returning
from the farms down the valley. Their legs shone with red
dust. One woman who walked alone carried on her head a
long cane basket filled with cassava and in her right hand
a hoe and a knife. A small girl trotted behind her. After a
while, the latter stopped and began to play with some ants.
The mother had gone many paces before she knew that her
daughter was not following. When she at last knew, she
came back and smacked the girl with the side of the
matchet blade. And while the child howled she lifted her
up with the left hand, cradled her under her left armpit
and proceeded, laden all over.

'The day is running away,' said Okoli Mbe.

The sunlight had become lazier and lazier and at last departed altogether. Night was creeping in steadily and the
surrounding bush was making a final mournful stir before
turning in. From somewhere the guinea-hen was shouting
to her mate to return.

'Okwai! Okwai!'

But the guinea-cock was not yet ready for home. 'Nje . . .

nje . . . nje jeli ulu! Nje . . . nje . . . jeli ulu! Should I go and steal for you? Leave me alone.'

'We must go now,' said Nnoli Nwego. 'We will come back tomorrow.'

They went.

Danda was alone. And he didn't like it. The night had crept menacingly close, blotting away the lineaments of quick life, transforming them into ragged menacing ghosts. Danda sought activity, to keep his eyes away from the void. Earlier in the day Okoli Mbe had brought him some yams, a cooking pot and a tripod stand. Nnoli had come that evening with live charcoals in a potsherd. Danda now shoved in some splices of wood between the stands, laid the charcoals underneath and blew on them. A tongue of flame shot up and a small circle was reclaimed from the darkness. Danda cleaned the pot, poured water in it and put it in the fire. But just at this moment a heavy wind came from somewhere in the night and threatened the fire. Danda was afraid. For if the fire went out there was no other means of making a fresh one; the village was far away and besides was cut off by the vibrating darkness. Danda knelt hastily and countered the wind with his breath. The struggle lasted a short while and at the end Danda won. Happy, he cut up the yams, washed and dropped them into the pot . . .

Outside in the night the crickets had risen, and been chanting nocturnes. There were two choirs. The first sang and the other responded.

> Uwa amaka (The world is good.)
> Eziokwu? (True word?)
> Uwa amaka
> Eziokwu?

Danda listened to them and watched the shadows that played grotesquely on the wall of the house.

Soon the yams were done. Danda fed, dipping the slices of yam into a plate of palm oil.

Now that he had nothing more to do he was suddenly

aware of the darkness. In the woods nearby the owl was welcoming the spirits into man-land.

Ukwu—u—kwu—u—oho o-o! Ukwu-u-kwu-u oho—o-o! Danda was a little afraid. He took up his flute and endeavoured to exorcize the lurking spirits but didn't succeed. So rising, he fled to the mud bed in the living room, lay down and wrapped himself up. But he could still hear the spirits as they circled and stamped about in the gloom of the woods. They seemed to be playing some kind of blind game. One young dead was blindfolded and the others capered round daring him to find them.

'Sofi,' the blind spirit called.

'Nno,' the others taunted.

'Sofi.'

'Nno.'

Danda closed his eyes and eagerly sought sleep. But at the same time the spirits were coming into the house. There was a leader who had two heads and eyes of fire, then a dwarf whom his companions called onye oya—the sick one —one of his limbs was missing.

'Give him your leg,' a wiry spectre said to Danda.

'Yes, give him your leg.'

'I won't,' said Danda. He wanted to rise and flee but couldn't, a heavy weight seemed to pull him down.

'Cut his leg for me, do,' shouted the ghostly dwarf.

'Yes, give him your leg.'

The chief spirit crept nearer and stretched his hand to snatch it. But at the same time Danda grew wings and slowly floated over the heads of the spirits and above the oji trees and the red and green streams below them.

With a bubble of delight the spirits followed. At first they jostled and tottered on the ground gesturing comically at their flying quarry. Then they also grew wings and floated after him.

Many years passed. They crossed seven lands, seven seas, they crossed the blood river where the sun was born and where it was given its red pigment.

The spirits still came after. And now Danda found he

was making no progress, the spirits would get him. They were on him and many things were happening at once.

'Hold him.'

'Hold him.'

'Cut his leg.'

'Yes, cut his leg.'

But mixed with these cries were the voices of men murmuring freshly in the early dawn, borne down by a muffled wind that whispered the mysteries of a new-born day. The guinea-hen had awakened, too, and was rousing her mate.

Okwai! Okwai!

The guinea-cock was annoyed and roared that he would sleep some more.

'Nje nje jeli ulu? Nje—nje—jeli ulu! Leave me alone!' These sounds, perhaps because they were washed by the morning dews, emerged wet and clean. But they were not as reassuring to Danda's ears as the childish treble of big Nnoli Nwego and the loud bass of small Okoli Mbe. The latter wore a big pair of shorts and a military khaki jacket for a shirt on top of it.

'Hoa!' piped Nnoli. 'The day is born.' He carried two hoes with new handles over his shoulder. 'Your mother says we should give them to you. She got them out of your hut.'

Danda took the hoes and examined them critically. He had been making them for some six months, adding little touches whenever the fancy was on him. This was the way he worked at his blacksmithing. Once in a while he would shut himself up and work pell-mell all day on a spear or knife. Then for months after that he would not touch them or would only at intervals make slight adjustments. The hoes that Nnoli brought were finished and ready for market.

'They will give us palm wine in the market this evening . . .'

'Do you think old Ebenebe would be at home now?' asked Danda, rising from the raised mud and yawning.

'No, as we were coming we saw him going to work. Why do you want him?'

'We want to get some mats from him. It may rain and the roof is rotten.'

The other two looked up at a depression on the roof through which a shaft of the morning sunlight was shooting . . .

'You want to buy the mat from Ebenebe?'

'No, ask him to give me them.'

'You are not fit,' said Nnoli, laughing.

'We shall see.'

They set out and soon got on to the footpath which led from the farms to the village. After a while the road entered a grove of palms and the three men now walked single file, Okoli Mbe leading the way and Danda bringing up the rear.

'But let me ask you,' said Okoli Mbe, 'to whom does Ebenebe want to leave his wealth when we look for him and do not see him?'

'Only the spirits know!'

There was deep silence in the grove except for the sound the men made as they swished away the grass which had overgrown the road.

The compound when they came to it was fenced in by carefully thatched outer walls. Inside the walls was a grass hut behind which stretched a long well-filled barn. The gate was locked tight.

'The back of the compound will be better,' said Okoli Mbe. On the other side of the compound there was a thick jungle of plantains.

'You stay here, Nnoli, and watch,' said Danda. 'We shall go round.'

They began to detour round to the back.

'There is no dog?' asked Okoli Mbe.

'Ebenebe does not keep dogs,' whispered Danda. 'But I am told he sets traps.'

They had to step cautiously to avoid the traps and also the thorns that had fallen from the orange tree nearby. A little while later they entered the banana grove.

'Now then,' said Danda. He bent down. Okoli Mbe

lightly skipped on his shoulder, and using this as a spring-board leapt over the wall and into the compound. He was a long time and Danda was becoming worried.

'Is it well?' he asked over the wall.

'Sh!' a voice said from the other side. 'Don't ring your bells.' Danda remembered but as he stepped back from the wall the bells tinkled again.

'Sh!' admonished the same voice.

A moment later, the call of a bird was heard coming from the direction of the gate. Soon after that the door was heard opening, making a nervous, crackling noise with its hinges.

'Come out!' Danda whispered urgently.

There was no reply. Years passed. And then Danda suddenly sensed that somebody was behind him. He didn't dare turn round for fear his bells would invite others. Whoever was behind was taking his time creeping noiselessly up.

'He has returned home,' said Nnoli Nwego's voice near Danda's ears.

'Did he see you?'

'Yes. He asked me what I was doing near his house. I told him I was watching the birds.'

'Hai,' laughed Danda.

'Sh!' said Nnoli. 'Your bells.'

'He will catch Okoli Mbe?'

'Yes.'

They waited. After some time the door of the gate creaked close.

'He hasn't caught him.'

'Ngwa!' whispered a voice from the compound. Two attanis were held over the wall. Danda received them. Some more were on the way and Nnoli helped them over. There were now twenty attanis outside. Then Okoli Mbe's voice was heard saying: 'Pick me up!' Nnoli stretched over the wall and levered him up.

'He didn't catch you?' said Danda.

'No, I hid in the barn . . . I can't understand why a man should go about jingling like a newly-married lady. Yes, I had to go into the barn. And ask me what I saw?'

'Yams.'

'True word. Look.' He pointed to a swelling at his groin. 'What is it?'

Okoli Mbe untied a knot and revealed the tumour as a collection of yams.

'Ahai!'

'Let's go.' Nnoli lifted the mats to his head and Danda came after him. Okoli Mbe trotted behind trying to hush the chattering bells.

They didn't dare take the road as many people were going through it to the farms. Instead they made a detour round it. This involved pushing through unpathed wood festooned in many places by lianas.

They reached the hut at last and set about repairing the roof. First they made a ladder by strapping short clubs to two bamboo posts. With it Nnoli climbed on to a series of posts stretched across the inner room, serving as a ceiling. Danda cut a frond from a small palm nearby and stripped off the leaves. Then he split it half-way down the middle. From his place inside Nnoli would push up an old but intact attani which overlapped another that had rotted. Then he would untie the latter and it would slither down. Danda who stood outside would fork up with the frond a fresh attani and insert it in the opening—Nnoli would take hold of the head of this new attani and thatch it to the bamboo framework.

Meanwhile Okoli Mbe had set about preparing the yams for breakfast. He gathered straw and some faggots, then took out a box of matches from the pocket of the military jacket. 'It is what makes the world of the white man wonderful,' he said before striking the match. 'Things are so easy.'

By the time the other two men had finished work the yam was well roasted. Okoli Mbe went out and cut a leaf of a plantain. The food was spread on its broad surface. Then the three of them set on it dipping the slit blades into a clay plate full of palm oil. When it was all over, Nnoli sighed.

'We have no palm wine.'

'When we sell the hoe we shall drink,' said Okoli Mbe picking his teeth with his forefinger and thumb.

For a few minutes after this they sighed and yawned in a lazy-satisfied mood. Then Nnoli said:

'Did you hear? Ekeama Idemmili has gone away.'

'Gone away?' cried Danda interested.

'Yesterday evening she was about, laughing and jumping in her usual way. Nobody would have suspected her of waiting to do anything crooked. But early this morning she left, taking all that belonged to her.'

'Ahai,' said Danda.

'That means you can now go home,' said Nnoli.

'Woman that is handsome!' said Danda. 'Nwokeke cannot now bring the case up.'

'Go home? No. Unless something spoils.'

'Ahai!' said Nnoli.

Okoli Mbe had been looking very thoughtful. At last he gave vent to his thoughts.

'Something has been troubling me. People in my age group have married and begot children. I am still alone. Is it not time to think about what I should do with my world?'

His companions were nonplussed by his scruples. Nnoli didn't know what to say and rubbed down his Adam's apple. Danda cleaned his flute.

In the village, people were beginning to stir for the market. Many men were heard arousing their friends by whistling to them in the manner of birds.

'Let's go,' said Danda. He gathered his hoes and stood up. The others rose too and they set out.

The first group of people to greet Danda in the market were the women who besieged him for his hoe.

'Rain,' they all cried.

'Daughters of beauty!' Danda was himself again. He had come into his element surrounded by people, women. His eyes sparkled and his features were very expressive.

'Hoa!' he bawled.

The demand for hoes at this time of the year was very great and there was a struggle for Danda's, which the women knew were usually cheap and fine.

'Five shillings each of them,' said Danda, 'and bitter-leaf soup for a market week in addition.'

The bargaining took off from there. And the women finally succeeded in beating down the price of each hoe to two shillings and only a course of bitter-leaf soup.

But none of them had any money—at least they said they hadn't. They promised to pay later. The course of bitter-leaf soup Danda could have whenever he visited their houses.

'It is well, my wives,' said Danda smiling.

'You won't see the face of that money,' said Okoli Mbe, after the women had gone away.

'I know,' said Danda. 'They smile in my face but as soon as my back is turned they say: "Do not take notice of Danda. He is no good." But I will not tell you a lie, son of our fathers. I cannot run away from the smile of a woman. Let us go for palm wine.'

CHAPTER FIFTEEN

It was old Imedu that told me the story and with a great deal of sly glee.

'Yes, son. I didn't know a man could cut up so nasty about a few attanis . . . Well this was how it was. We were sitting in the ogwe early that morning looking round to see if we could have a few cups when Ebenebe dashed in.

' "I will deal with him," he roared.

' "Who?" we asked.

' "That scamp, Akumma Nwego." '

It is difficult to say why Ebenebe attributed the theft of his attanis to Akumma Nwego. It is true that the previous day he had seen Akumma's brother, near his house in suspicious circumstances. And perhaps the logical thing would have been to go to Nnoli. But Ebenebe preferred to go to Akumma. Apparently he argued in this way: every Aniocha man knows that Akumma is a rogue. Nobody as yet had accused his brother so if the latter was seen near my place it would be his brother who had brought him.

'I will show him.' Ebenebe spoke in a nervous high pitched voice, emphasizing his points with energetic gestures. Four of the fingers of his right hand had been deformed from childhood and as he raised them they appeared like the fingers of a wooden Ikenga.

He was a little gnome of a man with small, sharp eyes and a dry, parched face. His neck was thin, leathery and bent permanently sideways so that he walked like a crab.

He had no family and had lived alone for sometime. And because of this many stories had been going around in our town about him. Some said that he had murdered his father and that since then the spell of the Alusi had been on him. Others said that in the old days he had sold a virgin into slavery.

Personally I had never believed any of these stories. I suspected that people told them out of envy. For Ebenebe was a very wealthy man. He had a large flock of sheep and goats. His trees produced the heaviest fruit of the year. These trees made him more enemies than the alus he was alleged to have committed. For on days when the fruit was to be plucked many villagers would come to help themselves, each of them providing himself with a pocket hidden somewhere on his body. But at the end of the picking Ebenebe would discover all the hiding places and rescue his stolen ube. Sharp, cautious and hardworking, that was Ebenebe. It was not easy to over-reach him as many an Aniocha loafer would admit to his cost.

'Ebenebe cried on for some time,' continued Imedu, 'and ended with: "If Akumma has swallowed those twenty mats I will make him vomit them."

'"True word," we said.'

It wasn't that they were very fond of Ebenebe who had a reputation for being difficult, but they thought it would be fun to watch the encounter between him and the village prize idler. So a few rose from the ogwe, beat their bottoms to clear their cloaks of dust, and followed behind Ebenebe.

As they went on down the main road many people would stop them and ask what the matter was. Ebenebe would tell them. 'True word,' they would say too and join the group. By the time Ebenebe reached Akumma's compound he had with him a sizable number of supporters. Akumma Nwego, pulling at his charred pipe, squatted on the top of the steps before the gate of his compound. A long matchet lay beside him. He had been meaning to go to work that morning but had not been able to overcome his laziness. The fight with this weakness was a daily occurrence and it was seldom that Akumma won.

He now faced the mob with his habitual calm.

'Where are my attanis?' Ebenebe asked.

'Your attanis? What happened to them?'

'Question! (Ajuju!) He is questioning me, people of our land.'

Ebenebe turned and invited the others to share his scorn.

'What did you do with my attanis, akalogholi?'

'Nothing,' said Akumma Nwego smiling and pulling harder at the pipe. 'I gave them away to Nwanyeocha the mad woman.'

'So you think we have come to laugh? Get out of my way.' Ebenebe darted forward to get into the compound. Akumma Nwego's knife flashed once and Ebenebe ducked. Too late. There was a cry of horror from the people.

'He has killed him.'

Not quite. Ebenebe had escaped death by inches.

'Akalogholi!' he shouted as he regained safety behind his followers. Akumma Nwego still held his murderous knife and was still unruffled.

'You will eat sand when we bring you before the chieftain.' Ebenebe killed his enemy with a deadly glance, and then stamped away with some of the crowd. The rest who were not satisfied with the abrupt way the action had ended remained behind gazing with great curiosity at Akumma Nwego.

'The old stick,' said the scamp, indicating with the tail of his pipe the departing Ebenebe. 'What is he waiting for? Why doesn't he die?'

The spectators were at first shocked by this sentiment. But as its full implication unfolded itself they were only struck by its truth. It was indeed true that Ebenebe was old, how old nobody knew.

The mob dispersed, chuckling to themselves.

CHAPTER SIXTEEN

The last guest had gone now and the numerous plantain leaves which had been used for sharing baked cassava had been cleared away. Onuma was left with his father. Both were satisfied but for different reasons. Araba was proud that his name in Aniocha had been enhanced. Onuma was pleased that he had won the approval of his father. Since boyhood he had never really liked Araba—there had never been much contact between them—but he had devoted his life to winning his good opinion. For this he had worked hard, suffered privations, eaten sparingly and saved every penny he could lay hold of. He remembered a day very long ago when Araba had beaten him hard and remarked:

'You won't come to much. Look at the boys in your age group. They are worthy of their fathers. But who conceived you?'

And now many years after that Araba had been forced to eat his words. Now he talked of nothing but of his so promising son. Onuma, young though he was, had now bought a hundred-pound wife and had for one week kept open house to his kindred and relatives. No person in the same age group could have done more.

But the cost of the achievement had been heavy. Onuma had barely enough money to pay for transport for himself and his wife. And when he got back to the town it would be like starting all over again. He would continue his timber trade. The peasants called him an oibo worker, in other words a clerk in a Government office. He hadn't corrected them for the name oibo worker carried greater prestige than trader and Onuma could use some lustre.

But the timber trade was not quite as profitable as it used to be. One of the reasons why Onuma had hastened home at the time he did was the fear that if he delayed longer the slump might force him to dip into his savings and in that way postpone indefinitely the day when he would show himself to Aniocha. And now what was he to do? He wished he could leave his wife at home when he went, and come for her when times were better. But he would have to find a very strong reason to satisfy Araba, a reason which would still make him retain his confidence in his so promising son.

To clear his head and also to take a last look at Aniocha he took a walk . . . After a while he reached the church and its sombre graveyard. There was nobody about and the old trees looked lonely, whistled mournfully. Onuma first looked in at a small mud-brick hut behind the church. This was the home of the priest but just now Father Royde was not in.

Onuma tip-toed into the empty church. The statue of the Virgin dominated the altar and in whatever place you stood she smiled directly at you. She seemed very much alive, not a thing of marble but a woman of warm flesh and blood.

Pictures of the Passion littered the wall and were also very real. Onuma contemplated almost with a shiver the officers of Pilate that were knocking thorns into Christ's head. He was awakened from his reverie by the rat-tat of a motor-cycle and the screams of children. He ran out of the building and saw Father Royde.

The priest was surrounded by a group of eager, young children some of whom pushed the bicycle while others gambolled round it. Father Royde, smiling, picked his way between the numerous eager feet. At first he did not look Onuma's way. Onuma approached with reluctance. As he came near, Father Royde looked up and smiled.

The children had stopped at the threshold of the small hut. Father Royde took the motor-cycle, braced himself, and carried it into the building. Then he came out again and dismissed the children.

'Come in,' he beckoned to Onuma.

They faced each other seated on stools, around a small, compact table.

'You are one of the sons of Chief Araba Udeji?'

'Yes,' Onuma marvelled at the older man's memory. It must be ten years since they met.

'O yes, I remember you. You did so well at the test before your confirmation.'

Onuma himself had a vague recollection of the incident.

'Your brother, Danda the singer, gave us some trouble early this year . . . He joined the church and then suddenly ran away.'

'It is Danda's way,' said Onuma with a smile.

'I hope he will come back again. I like him. I like him very much . . . Well how have you got on?'

Onuma told him.

'Timber trading. That's a fine job. They say they make much money in it.'

'Some people do.'

Father Royde smiled and then said: 'Let's see if there is anything to eat in this house.' He called 'Philip!'

A small boy of ten ran in from the small kitchen at the back of the house.

'Do we have some food in the house, Philip?'

'Only rice, Father.'

'Get us some. Two plates—one for my friend.'

Philip smiled recognition at Onuma and darted out. A moment later he returned, carrying two plates of rice. Father Royde took one and extended the other to his guest.

They fed in silence. At the end Philip cleared away. Then Father Royde resumed the talk.

He had the same healthy colour, the same thick wavy hair which Onuma remembered so well. His room had not changed much either. There were the usual three hard-backed chairs, the stiff table and an old shelf stocked full of books. The bedroom would not be any more luxurious. The hut was at first a one-room dwelling house but because people came to it at any time they liked, Father Royde, aiming at privacy, had one day with the help of one or two parishioners made a bedroom with a mud partition.

He now spoke to Onuma of the progress of the church, of the difficulties they had had to overcome. Then he suddenly asked: 'It was you who said you were going to be a priest, wasn't it?'

'Yes.' Onuma remembered the night ten years ago when he, a bright stripling, loitering with a friend near the white man's house, had been called to his saintly presence. He had given them sweets to still their trembling and then had asked them: 'What would you like to be when you leave school?'

'A priest,' Onuma had said. He had only answered then as small boys would do, what he thought would please his questioner. But now he thought it would not have been such a bad idea to enter the priesthood, wear a soft-snow-white cassock and officiate in the impressive ceremony of the bread and wine. Above all, be with Father Royde, who had always been his hero.

'It is not a bad job,' continued the priest rubbing his ruddy chin. And then he went on to tell how he himself had left a good job as a University teacher to come out to Africa to serve God. 'There is satisfaction in it. So long as one knows what one is doing.'

Onuma was very thoughtful as he rose to go.

'God bless you.' The priest made a sign of the cross over him. Onuma went.

He had got the solution to his problem pat. He would be a priest. But how would Araba take it?

Araba was stretched on the ojo fanning himself with his hand. It had sunned intensely during the day and now as evening was coming on all the heat which had accumulated on the ground began to rise and choke everybody. Onuma found a seat and as he sat down he unbuttoned his shirt and blew down it to cool his body.

'Your wife has come,' said Araba. 'Have you seen her?'

'No,' said Onuma.

Araba looked at him hard. 'It doesn't seem sweet to you? How you young ones behave is a mystery. When Nwamma came to me I danced all over Aniocha . . . And your wife is a good-looker too. Small, it is true, but a good-looker.'

'It is well.'

Araba gave it up with a shrug. After a short period of silence Onuma said: 'I went to see the white fada.'

'He is a friend,' said Araba. 'I like him . . . Did they tell you the story: he once took Danda into his church . . . But I said at that time that it would not last long. It did not . . .'

'He asked me if I would like to be a fada myself.[2]

'And you said yes?'

'Yes.'

'Why not. Any job that a white man does must be well paid. You will get more money from it than from your present job?'

'Fadas are not paid.'

'So? Why then do you wish to become one? How will you support your wife?'

'Priests don't marry. They live alone.'

Araba stared. Finally he said: 'You were laughing at me? You were being childish . . . ?[2]

Onuma said nothing.

Araba turned away as if in contempt. But after a time he turned back and said sternly: 'Don't do it again. I am an old man and not fit for child's things.'

'But, Araba, you don't understand!'

'That you want to be an akalogholi?'

'No.[3]

'Let me hear no more chicken talk.'

There was silence, sullen on the one hand and indifferent on the other. A moment later Okelekwu and other members of the kindred came into the obi to drink evening wine. Nwafo Ugo had just returned from hunting for he carried an old dane-gun in one hand and a dead nchi in the other.

'It might fetch four shillings in the market,' said a tapster.

'You don't,' said Nwafo. 'I won't take anything less than eight shillings for it.'

The wine was now served and while the men drank Araba related what Onuma had just told him. The kindred laughed.

'The type of things men do in this world,' muttered a herdsman.

'Let me hear it again,' said Nwafo. 'The boy doesn't want money, he doesn't want a wife, he doesn't want children?'

'That's what I hear, men of our land,' said Araba.

'Son of ours,' Nwafo patted Onuma kindly. 'If your father had been a fada and refused marriage how would you have come into the world?'

'It is the white man's trick,' said Okelekwu. 'The white man likes to throw sand into our eyes. Why does he try to persuade boys like that not to marry? Tell me. Why, because he wishes to keep us down. If our people increase, they will drive the white people out of this land of ours.'

'That's it,' said Araba with an impatient gesture. He had begun to feel uncomfortable at having other people barge into what should be strictly private to him.

There was general snuff after this and then Nwafo said:

'Wait, men of our lands, I heard something today. They tell me that the Ubili people have resumed their ancient alu.'

The Ubilis were a small pocket of men who lived at the outskirts of the ten towns. Because of their remoteness from Aniocha, they were by Aniocha people looked down upon as wild fellows, men of the backwoods.

'Which alu have they resumed?' asked Okelekwu, 'They were known for so many.'

'Eating the flesh of men.'

'So?'

'Yes,' said Okelekwu, 'it is true they used to eat the flesh of men. But that was hundreds of years ago. In the days of my great great grandfather the Ubilis used skulls as drinking cups. I have never thought much of the Ubili people. They have always been foolish, like goats. Nwafo, how did your story go?'

Nwafo shifted his heavy bulk and smiled as one would say: 'I thought we would come to it at last.' He took his time over the story. With great deliberation he pushed into his nostrils a respectable-sized lump of snuff and sighed happily with the callousness of a man who has something that others want.

'Yes,' he said at last. 'The Ubili people have resumed their old alu.'

'What did they do? Ahai! Some men cannot tell a story straight.'

Nwafo Ugo winked tolerantly at Okelekwu. 'Keep your wrapper on,' his good-humoured face suggested. 'I will tell this story in my own way, and I have all the time in the world to tell it in.'

'It was like this,' he said at last. 'A traveller from a land far away came to see his friend at Ubili. The friend welcomed him and on his behalf called many to come and drink . . . The feast went on all day. And then as night was coming down the friend gathered a few ruffians, set on the traveller and knocked him about. That was some welcome.' Nwafo stopped here to take snuff.

'What happened?' urged the herdsman.

'Wait, wait, don't be impatient. You will hear everything.'

After a triumphant minute he resumed:

'This morning the traveller appeared at the Police Station at Mbammili. His head was broken and his body was full of wounds. You know what had happened? The Ubili murderers after beating him senseless had taken him into the barn and left him for dead. Then they went to fetch straw with which to roast his body . . . But he wasn't dead. His strength was gone but his chi helped him over the wall of the barn and on to the oibo road from where a land-boat brought him to the Police Station at Mbammili.'

The Umunna digested the story and were impressed. But there was in Okelekwu's face an expression of scepticism. Most gossip from the ten towns came to Aniocha through him and he was jealous of this privilege. Accordingly after Nwafo Ugo's story he waved his cowtail doubtfully and said in a dry voice:

'You told the story so well. Were you present at the incident?'

Nwafo smoothed the doubter. 'I went to Mbammili this morning and saw the victim with these two eyes of mine.'

'Hai,' sighed a herdsman. 'The bushmen! After so many years to go back to their alu!'

'A people will always be what they have always been.'

'Sons of beasts.'

The night drew near and the men rose. But before they went they cautioned Onuma.

'Go well, my son. But remember, out there you are not working for yourself alone but for us too.'

'You and your like are the lucky ones,' said Nwafo Ugo. 'You eat the world. If I had read books I would now be equal to the white man. But I couldn't. My chi gave me a dry head.'

'Beware of men. It is no longer the spirits that kill men but other men. The world is bad nowadays.'

'Stuttering,' said Araba contemptuously, after the men had gone. 'How they talk. As if you were a child.' He snuffed for a while sneezing intermittently. Then he got up and went out himself.

Onuma walked to his house and began to pack. There would be nothing for it now but to take the wife with him. He hoped something would turn up. The box was half full when he sensed the presence of somebody. He looked back and saw his mother. She stood timidly by the door as if she were afraid to come in.

'You have come, Mother,' he said.

'So you will go tomorrow?'

'Yes.'

'I am afraid.'

'There is nothing bad that is.'

'Let me help you.' She took from him the shirt he was just packing and placed it in a better position in the box. 'Your wife has come,' she said.

'It is well.'

'Treat her well, she is well-behaved.'

'She will be all right.'

'What will you take on the way? Shall I pack akpu into the box?'

'No,' laughed Onuma. 'How can I carry akpu? I shall buy things on the way.'

'Is the food of strangers safe? Don't they poison it? Men of the world are bad nowadays.'

The box was full. Onuma took it from her, locked it. 'It is finished,' he said.

She stood aside constrained. Onuma spoke to her but she did not reply. She stood about for a time and then walked away . . .

Araba also came to Onuma's hut that night. He was drunk and, as his wont when he was in that condition, he began to boast.

'Some fool has just told me that he had the ozo before me. I told him he was stuttering.'

'Yes.'

'Let them all come . . . I had eaten the ozo meat several years before that poor fool. And you will eat it too. Do you hear what I say. You will eat the ozo meat and be an ozo man yourself . . . You will call Aniocha men and they will have so much to eat that they won't see their way home. Let them all—' the rest of this challenge ended in a tipsy mutter after which Araba swayed about for some minutes and finally steadied himself by holding to the well . . . 'You go tomorrow?' he said at last.

'I have just packed.'

'That's it.' Araba stretched and yawned. 'Go then, openly, and fear nothing. God who created the world'—Araba staggered winefully away, crooning a masquerade song . . .

'Me, an ozo,' Onuma thought, amused. How was Araba to know that the ozo was forbidden by the church?

CHAPTER SEVENTEEN

Seeing Onuma off was again the collective business of the umunna. They were joined by relatives from the other villages. The number was further swelled by outsiders who had stopped on their way to work, to chat. Araba presided over the whole group. Occasionally he would take Onuma aside to give him final instructions.

'I don't feel at ease about you. You haven't got any ogwu to protect you.'

'I am all right, Araba.'

'You should have taken that ogwu I made some years ago. So far it has kept the whole compound whole. But you tell me the church forbids it. Many church men nowadays use ogwu. You cannot church more than the fada—'

'Nothing will spoil,' said Onuma. He was a little impatient. In the time of waiting he stood apart from his family glancing with distaste at his wife.

A lean, small girl with undeveloped breasts but a pretty face. She was excited by her prospects and danced and wriggled about. When girls of her age passed by she became self-conscious.

'She will be a big missis in no time,' said Nwamma. 'When she returns she will turn her nose.'

The mother of the girl smiled and stood up to smooth her new dress.

'You must work, my friend,' said Chinwe with mock roughness. 'You shouldn't stay in your house making yourself beautiful.'

'There will be no time for beautifying. Children will come.'

The girl on hearing this turned sharply to her husband. She was still afraid of him.

Immediately after this a lorry came by. Nwamma waved

to it to stop but the driver drove past.

'You don't know how to stop them,' said Okelekwu. 'Let me take the next one.'

Okelekwu's praise name was Onye ije—he who travels. And he had won this title because of some mysterious journeys he used to make in the dry season. The people he visited were said to be foolish, like goats. When he came among them Okelekwu spoke in dibia-like language. The men conceived great awe for him. They asked him their fortunes and brought their sick to be healed. In return they loaded Okelekwu with gifts. The result would be that Okelekwu returned to Aniocha at the end of the dry season, rich, and for the rest of the year while others sweated in the farms he sat on the ogwe at the market place taking snuff and hashing up new proverbs.

In spite of all his authority, however, many lorries still ignored him.

'They are arrogant,' he said. 'As if we cared. Let them all go by.'

'The road is crowded today,' said fat Nwafo Ugo. 'Get me a pad quickly, let me carry this one.' He pointed to a small car going by, occupied by a white man and his wife. The other villagers laughed. It must be a poor white who could not afford a bigger land-boat.

A few moments later a closely packed lorry rattled to a stop.

'Ida, who is going?' asked a young man—tight trousers, a T-singlet on which was painted the picture of a girl, all breasts and legs, and American accent picked up from the cinemas.

'Two people for Ida,' said Okelekwu.

'And all this load here?'

'There is not much load.'

'Okay, get in.'

'No, wait.' Okelekwu would handle this his way. 'How much?'

'Oh,' said the brash young man. 'Ten shillings for each of them, and five shillings for the load. Twenty-five shillings.'

'Impossible,' said Okelekwu. 'Last month when I travelled to Ida—'

'Are we now to listen to fables?' cried the passengers in the lorry. 'Don't waste our time, man.'

'We shall pay you twenty shillings,' Okelewu said to the young man.

'Twenty shillings. Perhaps you think we run this lorry in order to show our merciful hearts?'

'I didn't say you did. Twenty shillings. Not an anini more. Take it or go.'

'Your head must be turned,' shouted brash. He struck the tailboard with his fist and roared: 'Go on!' As the lorry moved he looked back at Okelekwu and said: 'Bushman!'

'Tell that to your father, son of a beast!' said Okelekwu. 'Pride has filled the heads of the young. Ever heard such brashness?' he said to the kindred. 'And he asked for twenty-five shillings. If he had been making money so fast he would not still remain a servant. He would have built himself a two-storied iron house in his poor father's compound.'

'Twenty-five shillings,' said Onuma speaking for the first time. 'It is not too much.'

'It is,' said Okelekwu. 'We won't pay a penny more than twenty shillings. Indeed do we pay so much? When the next land-boat comes I am going to stand on nineteen shillings. Leave it to me, son. This is your father's town. If you don't travel today you can go back home and enjoy your mother's bitter-leaf soup.'

Another lorry came immediately after.

'Ida,' cried Okelekwu.

'It is well,' said the lorry's young man carelessly. 'Get in.'

'There are two people.'

'And all the loads?'

'Yes.'

'Get in.'

'How much does it cost? Nineteen shillings?'

'Very well, get in.'

'I said nineteen shillings?'

'Do you want to come with us or don't you?'

Okelekwu smiled triumphantly and waved his whisk.

'Put the loads in,' he ordered.

Everybody began to bustle. The young girl's mother suddenly leapt up and clasped her daughter.

'What is it?' she said wild-eyed. 'What do they want with her?'

The girl herself was impatient. She was far too happy to share her mother's grief at parting. 'Has anything spoilt, Mother?' she asked.

'What do they want with her?' cried the mother to the others.

'That's enough, woman,' said Araba.

The other women murmured: 'It kills the heart, yes indeed it does.'

Mgbeke was at a loss too. Too shy to go to her son she leaned on an ogbu tree and tried to prevent others from seeing her tears.

The loads had been piled in. Onuma and his wife entered and waved to their relatives; the lorry moved away.

'Where is he going?' said Mgbeke addressing the air, it seemed.

'They will return one day,' said the other women comforting her away. The mother-in-law stood for a time waving at the departing lorry. Then she turned back and walked home weeping and laughing. Some women who were passing by were heard asking: 'Is she mad?'

'It kills the heart indeed. Yes it does,' answered those who knew the cause of the woman's grief.

'Today's own business is ended,' said Araba rising from the ogwe. 'Some years hence he will come back and we shall see what his arms have achieved.'

'True word.' Those of the kindred who had some work to do got up and walked away with him. The others settled themselves more comfortably on the ogwe and searched their bags for snuff.

Only a month passed. Araba had been kept at home by bad weather. Since the morning the sky had been dark and heavy with clouds, and rain was expected. But towards the middle of the day the sun peeped out, smiling like a sick person. Araba came out of the obi and began to sharpen a yam knife on a flat stone in front of the ifejioku (yam god) shrine. His attention was so taken up by this job and his ears so engaged by the sharp rasps of the knife that he failed to hear the door of the gate open. When at last he looked up the crowd was almost on him.

In front was Onuma's wife. Behind her were some villagers, men and women, some carrying heavy loads on their heads.

'Is it well?' Araba said, alarmed but maintaining his composure. The wife halted before him and burst into tears.

'What is it?' said Araba.

'Let her weep,' said Nwamma, leading the woman to the obi. The crowd went after them. Araba still squatted near the stone for a few moments and then biting his lips he also went into the obi. The wife had laid her head on Nwamma's shoulder and was still weeping.

'It is enough,' many women said to her.

Araba continued to bite his lips and looked around with special vehemence.

Then little by little the girl recovered. She told her tale brokenly.

Two weeks after she and her husband arrived at Ida, Onuma suddenly left her. She waited anxiously for two weeks before the letter came. She was to take all their things and return to Aniocha. He wasn't coming back he had written. Enclosed in the letter was a message for Araba.

'Is that all?' said Araba, his voice registering relief. 'Where is that message?' he said harshly.

She dipped into a little handbag and brought out the note. One of the men who had come with her could read.

'What does it say?' Araba asked sternly.

It said: Onuma had no money to keep his wife. He had crossed into the French territories to look round for a good job. Would Araba take care of the girl for some time?

For a few moments Araba bit his lips thoughtfully and then said, for the benefit of the men present: 'Nothing has spoilt. As long as he is alive all will be well.'

'Yes,' agreed one of the men. 'Life is what we pray for. Wealth will follow.'

But after the men had gone Araba took up the letter, tore it into pieces and then walked to the farm. That day he worked harder than he had ever done.

CHAPTER EIGHTEEN

Nwamma came out of her hut dressed for market. She carried a broad calabash basin inside which was the fish to sell. Trading in this was her main occupation. But she made little out of it, for she allowed too much credit and listened too often to tales of misery told her by her customers.

'Where do they say Danda is now?' asked Araba.

'Eh?' Nwamma was surprised at the abruptness of the question. She hadn't expected that Araba would refer again to Danda.

'Is he still in Aniocha?'

'Yes,' said Nwamma. 'They tell me he lives in Mgbafo Ndulu's hut near the farms.'

'It is well,' said Araba indifferently.

But he knew that Nwamma would understand and send for Danda.

Not long after Nwamma's departure, Diochi came. He seemed worried.

'Is it well?' said Araba.

'It is about your palms. I couldn't bring you the pot of palm wine this morning.'

'True word. I wondered why.'

Diochi was the son of the youngest wife of Araba's father. He was only a little older than Danda, being born long after Udeji had aged and after Araba had married his first wife. Since childhood he had been handicapped by a little hump. To help him support himself Araba had given him all the family palms to tap. In return and gratitude Diochi would bring him a calabash of palm wine every day.

'There was a misfortune this morning,' said Diochi. 'I don't know why they always happen to me.'

'What is it?'

For two days Diochi had missed wine in one of his palms. So he wondered whether it was sick. But Nwoye Oka the tree-cutter whom he called to look at the tree assured him that it was fit.

'Then, why is it playing this trick?'

'I don't know.'

Diochi later talked it over with his wife. She agreed that something was wrong. 'It is a thing for the afa,' she said. 'Perhaps some evil man has cast a spell on the palm.'

Diochi cracked his knuckles bitterly. 'Why should somebody want to persecute me?' he asked. 'I have done no one wrong. Nobody can take sand from my footprints.' But he would see the dibia. The next day, therefore, early in the morning, he set off for Eziakpaka up the hills. But just before he entered the village he met Okelekwu.

'Nwayo bu ije?' he greeted.

'Nnanyelugo,' said Okelekwu. 'Are you going or returning?'

'Going.'

'Is it well?'

Diochi detailed his misfortunes.

Okelekwu waved his whisk thoughtfully for a time and then said: 'It does not look to me a thing for the afa.'

'Is that so?'

'You think that spirits are behind your trouble? What kind of spirit drinks palm wine?'

'I have never met nor heard of one.'

'That's it. It is a thing begun by man. It looks to me you should keep watch by your palms early in the morning.'

'It is true word,' said Diochi with enthusiasm. 'Why did I not think of it? You have spoken true word. I shall not go to the afa. For long they have been eating my money.'

'Yes, should a man spend all his life supporting dibias with his money?'

They walked back together, whispering the chief news

of the day. Nwora Otankpa had just announced that he would take the ozo title in the scorch season; some ozos had fallen out with each other and were to appear before the village court.

The cock had cried twice. Diochi sat below an akpaka tree overlooking his palm. The night trailed on slowly until Diochi began to wander and his head to nod somewhat.

He was awakened by the bite of a mosquito and in a moment was very alert. For as he looked down he could see a dark figure detach itself from the darkness, approach the palm, circle it with the ete and begin to climb. Diochi's first thought was to run away—perhaps the thief was a spirit—but Diochi nerved himself and stood his ground.

The spirit, or whatever it was, reached the top of the tree, transferred the contents of Diochi's calabash into the one he carried and began to descend.

Diochi's fear left him. Now, plucky as pepper, he leapt up, ran down the hillock and as soon as the thief was down he was on him. But before his blow came down he knew who the spirit was and sprang back in dismay.

'You, stealing?' he said.

'Stealing?' said Danda. 'Can a man steal what belongs to him?'

'Does it belong to you?'

'It is my father's.'

'There are other palms. Why don't you go and knock them open. You know that this is your father's because it is being tapped.'

'Stuttering,' said Danda striding off. A few yards away he broke into a masquerade song.

Diochi scratched his head and regarded the retreating figure for some time. Finally he summed him up in one telling word: 'Akalogholi!'

'That's how it is,' Diochi murmured ruefully to Araba. 'But why did you let him take the wine away. Are you a woman?'

'I am not a woman,' said Diochi aroused, defiant. 'I am not a woman.'

Araba saw he had gone too far and kept silent.

'Why should I stop him? He is your son. He owns the palms as much as you. When we look for you and don't see you he will be the one to carry your ofo and cover the walls of your compound.'

Araba snorted.

'Ahai,' murmured Diochi. He took out his snuff box, knocked it several times on his knees, opened it, took a pinch and sighed harshly, pointedly. 'Trying to come the high hand over me,' he thought. 'It is not done!' Then before his fierceness would wear off he rose and strode off home. Outside the gate he scratched his head happily. His rather mousy eyes opened wide in a smile. For the first time in his life Diochi had asserted himself.

'He won't come back!' roared Araba as soon as Nwamma returned from the market.

'Has something happened?' Nwamma saw at once that he was in one of his periodic, terrible fits of rage. Whenever he was in that condition it could be fatal to cross him.

'What have you in that calabash?' he asked.

'Fish,' she said, trembling.

'Fish . . . fish . . . fish. Bring it here.'

Nwamma gave him the basket. He chose from it the choicest bit and crammed it into his mouth, glaring at Nwamma with bloodshot eyes. He wasn't really hungry, Nwamma saw, but to eat the fish was a way of working off his anger. He went on eating one morsel after another until Nwamma was moved to protest.

'The fish was bought with money and is for sale.'

'So?'

'Whatever you eat you will have to pay for.'

'I will pay!' shouted Araba beside himself. 'I will pay you and send you away from my obi.' He lifted the calabash, poured the contents on the floor and danced on them until they had all been squashed to bits. Then he tossed the calabash on the ground and smashed it.

'I will pay you,' he said, gasping with his exertion.

Nwamma gazed on the ruin with dismay. Then she turned on Araba and said calmly:

'Is there any more alu you want to make?'
'Your son will never see the inside of my house.'
'He will!'
'What's that?'
Nwamma kept silent.
'He will come back tomorrow.'
'I will kill you!' roared Araba.
But a knife was not available. A heavy pestle was, how-
ever, and Nwamma got at it first, raised it aloft and brought
it down hard on Araba's head. Blood spurted lo-lo-lo-lo to
the roof and Araba went down and cold.

Nwamma uttered a sharp, nervous cry and fled to her
hut.

And Araba might have bled to death. But Nwamma's cry
had brought Chinwe to the obi. She ran back to her hut
and fetched water and black soil. Then she washed the
wound with the one and stenched it with the other. Before
she had finished Nwamma had returned and was gazing at
Araba with horror. Some two or three women came out
too and surrounded her. Together they led her into her
hut and settled her down on the mud bed.

There, between sobs and hysterical laughter, she told
them how Araba had knocked her about, and pointed to
certain areas of her body which were smarting with the
wounds.

'I did nothing to him. He wants to kill me for nothing.'
The women consoled her. But they were also alarmed and
amazed at her hysterics. She had always been the one for
calm, the person to whom the other women brought their
troubles. And now she was crying like a child.

They stayed with her until she had calmed down a
little and then went away shaking their heads.

Early the next day Nwamma knelt before Araba. She
carried in her hand a calabash on which was a cock, its
legs tide together, two fresh eggs, and three cola seeds.
Araba took the cock, cut its throat with a small knife, and
poured the blood on the Ikenga.

Then the couple began to talk of many domestic matters.
It was then agreed that Danda should return.

CHAPTER NINETEEN

And when he came home it was to assume his heritage, the headship of the Araba compound. Araba had often said to Danda: 'Fate will catch up with you.' Fate was catching up with him. Two market weeks after he returned his father was laid low with a severe illness.

Not having ever known illness, at least as long as he could remember, he was frightened when it came.

'I am strong!' he shouted. 'I cannot die.' His eyes were fiery, his body rained sweat. 'I will not—' he sprang up in delirious fury but collapsed back to the bed muttering feebly. The men who had gathered round the bedside exchanged mournful glances. They did not feel as optimistic as Araba about his chances of recovery. For his was no ordinary illness. Fever first weakened your bones and kept you at home for a day or two before it put you to bed. But on the day Araba caught it he had risen in the morning strong and fresh. He had gone to the farm to harvest his yams and had carried home a large basketful. That night he had eaten a large supper prepared by two of his wives. But immediately after that he had fallen down and become very ill.

That was no fever. Perhaps Araba had sworn false by the Alusi and the god was claiming his life as a penalty for the alu. Many people refused to believe this. Araba was an honest man, they said. He didn't speak with two mouths. When he said yes, it was yes.

Then perhaps there was amosu in it. Someone who had eaten the amosu ogwu was wreaking malice on Araba, had changed himself into the drinker of blood and was now every night sucking him dry. An enemy had perhaps taken sand from his footprints, had mixed it with poison and left it beside the tree of evil in deep night when the worst spirits walked? A bad dibia may have been hired to make an effigy of Araba and prick it to death with poisoned darts?

The umunna shivered with fear as they whispered the news into the ears of other friends.

'There is evil everywhere, son of our fathers. Nobody is safe nowadays.'

—'It is no longer the spirits that kill men but other men. The world is becoming worse and worse to live in.'

—'Hai! We can only bow our heads to Chineke Olisaebuluwa who lives in the sky.'

Araba had no doubt who the enemy was. In one of his moments of lucidity, after visitors had gone from the Obi he had said to Nwamma:

'When I recover, I will deal with Nwokeke.'

'It is he?'

'I will deal with the tortoise—'

A dibia was immediately sent for. He came the next day. An old man with bristles of white beard all over his face, a shiny head, eyes ringed with blue and white clay. He was himself the epitome of magic. Squatting on the ojo he dipped into a smoky goatskin bag for the fetishes which made up his oracle; the ofo, tough and bloody-spattered, two other minor gods, a tortoise shell, pieces of white clay and two camwood coloured chains made of rows of cowries strapped together.

He began the ritual by breaking cola. Then he asked for some money with which to wash the faces of the divining spirits. He was given sixpence. Then in an awful voice he intoned a prayer first to the god of the sky, then to Araba's ancestors and finally to evil spirits whom he asked to keep away.

The dibia's bitter-sweet voice, the solemnity of the incantation closed over the obi like the wings of night. The audience, a few members of the Uwadiegwu umunna, bowed under the spell.

'What do you want to know? My afa is listening to you, woman.'

Nwamma shook herself free of the spell and said: 'Ask the spirits why this compound is dark. Are the eyes of our fathers open?'

The dibia drew two parallel lines on the floor. Lifting the two cowrie chains, he flung them down. One chain lay almost exactly on the line on the left.

'Left is for evil,' said the dibia. 'There is evil here.'

'Who has caused it?'

'Where is the source of the evil?' repeated the dibia. 'Where is it? Tell us, strong one, the dried meat that fills the mouth. Who has brought fire into this compound?'

'Man or spirit?'

'Man or spirit?' repeated the dibia, his eyes very alert. He raised the cowrie chains again and carelessly let them fall.

'The head of the evil cowrie points to man,' he said. 'It is a man who has brought fire into your compound.'

'Who is he?'

'Who is he? Tell us, strong one. Akweke, the egg of the holy snake which one breaks at one's peril.' He gazed at the deities on the floor, then looked up and darted searching glances at the kindred. For a moment his eyes held Nwokeke's. The two men measured each other then the dibia turned away.

'Shall we bring the sticks?' said Nwamma, guessing the dibia's thoughts.

'Yes, bring the sticks.'

Nwamma beckoned to Okelekwu and they walked out, stopping only when they were out of earshot.

Then Nwamma whispered: 'I thought of Nwokeke.'

'Yes,' agreed Okelekwu, sadly.

'And Idengeli. We had a quarrel with his wives over a strip of land.'

'No,' mused Okelekwu. 'Rule out Idengeli. He cannot do evil.'

'I don't know. I don't know anything.'

'Can you not think of any other person?'

'Yes . . . Ugoji went to the ulonabo, with Araba last month. Do you think it could be him?'

'It may be. You never know. Let us add him.'

From the thatch on the wall Nwamma broke off two

lengths of reed straw. One she named Nwokeke and the other Ugoji.

'It is well,' said Okelekwu. 'I will remember which is which.'

They went back to the dibia and presented him with the two straws. He promptly chose Nwokeke.

Okelekwu and Nwamma exchanged knowing glances.

'That enemy has power,' said the dibia. 'But we will overcome it with our own power. What do you say, my strong one?' He raised the ofo and struck it twice on the tortoise shell. 'There is all the power you need here. You must call a dibia who knows his job. Give him a goat and a cock and he will open the eyes of our ancestors. Call me if you like. I don't wish to boast, but no ogwu has resisted me so far.'

All those present nodded, impressed.

The dibia went.

Danda had not been at home when the dibia came; he had gone to Obunagu to collect certain roots which somebody had sworn were the only cure for Araba's illness. And as soon as he returned Idengeli drew him aside.

'Listen. People think that they know things but they know nothing. You have been advised by far too many ignorant people and you have been going east and west, wasting your time. There was a dibia who came today and one could see that he knows about ogwu no more than Akumma Nwego. Listen here, there is only one dibia who will make Araba live. She is a woman too, Mmankwo Nwadibia of Eziakpaka.'

'Very well,' said Danda. 'I will think about it.'

'Do not just think about it. Go now. Tonight, if possible.'

'Yes, I will go tomorrow.'

But the next day many other people suggested more important and more knowledgeable dibias to be consulted. Danda had to go to these.

That night tired, footsore, his bells dusty and plaintive, he trailed back home. Idengeli awaited him.

'And so you have not called Mmankwo Nwadibia of Eziakpaka?'

'There was no time. I walked to Mbammili, Agbenu, my head is heavy.'

'Don't say I didn't warn you. If Araba dies I shall have something to say to you—'

And yet neither dibias nor ogwus were any good for Araba. Sacrifices were held—many of them—the spirits of ancestors came, drank lots of blood and libations, but could not save their son. The compound was ringed with charms in vain. Nothing seemed able to break the power of the medicine that was taking Araba to the land of the spirits. The end was near. One night a complication set in in the form of a hard, prolonged hiccup which attacked Araba at intervals.

The next morning all who were related to Araba were sent for. His sisters married in other towns; those sisters' husbands, sons and daughters; fathers and mothers-in-law, accompanied by their friends. Most Uwadiegwus came too. The obi was full and the rest of the people overflowed into the yard. Through the whole day they waited and by evening were weary.

The hiccup had gone down and Araba now breathed very feebly. He would go home with the day.

The relatives, wearing that expression of dumb incomprehension and fear which people wear in the presence of death murmured in undertones.

—'The owl said "Ozumgbo" last night.'

—'It was a bad night, an evil night.'

—'They say Nwafo Ugo met a ghost.'

—'They say it is a man who is killing Araba.'

—'True, the world is bad.'

—'I am afraid. I am afraid of men.'

—'I am afraid of death, the way it attacks.'

—'No matter how strong a man is, when death comes, chololom! he goes.'

'Man is little, with a sound, fium! he dissolves like sand.'

'The journey is long.'

The road to spirit-land passes seven lands, seven seas, seven plains, seven deserts. The stopping places include where the sun was born and where it was bathed with blood, the home of the maimed who had lost their lives by violence, and finally led to the home of the old woman who gave the travellers spirit food which sets the mark of no return on their foreheads. Araba reached the old spirit's hut but there stopped his ears, bound his head with akwala string and refused to eat the food. He would not cross the line that divided spirits from men for if he did that Nwokeke would triumph.

The next dawn broke on weary, sleepy-eyed watchers. They were rising to depart when Araba opened his eyes and swore.

And two days later he was up, angry and dogmatic. It took him two market weeks to recover completely. At the end of that time he held a feast for the umunna to celebrate his recovery. And he enjoyed the feast all the more when he saw that Nwokeke did not attend.

Araba's preoccupation after that illness was how to make sure that Nwokeke would not be in a position to harm him again. He could of course have made some deadly nsi against him, a vengeance that would have been justified. But Araba shrunk from such a course, he remembered that he had sworn before the Alusi that he would never harm an umunna man. Besides nsi was a two-edged weapon that cut back to the man who wielded it.

So Araba took only protective measures. He sent for five famous dibias. They stayed with him for one market week and, as the saying goes, kneaded him in ogwu, and assured him that he was indestructible.

Still, when he met Nwokeke on the way the next day he could not bring himself to accept the congratulatory hand which the latter was on the point of offering. Nwokeke withdrew the hand just in time and before it had reached the point where a rebuff would have been apparent.

'Son of our fathers,' he said frowning and laughing. 'You are fit again.'

'Yes.'

'The eyes of your fathers must indeed be open.'

They stood together for a few minutes more, and talked about indifferent topics. But after they parted they knew now that there was a serious breach between them, perhaps irreconcilable.

Nwokeke, like Araba, took steps to protect himself. His own dibias came and for days the smoke of burnt offerings billowed from his obi.

The enmity inevitably came into the open. For Nwokeke once again demanded that the Uwadiegwu ozala should be brought to his compound. Three strong young men were to go to Araba and if possible force him to yield the trophy.

Araba awaited them in his obi. His eyes which had turned yellow after the fever were now a dangerous pink. Every now and then the calves in his short legs would shiver.

The door of the gate opened and he looked up and almost jumped out of his seat but when he saw who it was he subsided.

As soon as Chinwe came in, some instinct told her that something was wrong. She looked round and saw Araba and recognized the mood which he was in, it was the mood for murder. At first she hesitated and wondered if she could have done anything to put him in such a state. Finally concluding that she was innocent she walked on, though a little nervously. As soon as she had gone past him she tossed her head defiantly.

Safe in her own yard, she walked to the wall which separated her from Nwamma and looked over.

'Whom does our lord want to kill this time?' she asked.

'Kill?' Nwamma stopped mid-way in the act of putting salt into a soup pot that cooked on tripod stands erected temporarily in the middle of the compound. 'Did you say kill?'

'Yes. There is murder in his eyes.'

'So? A message came that he should return the family ozala to Nwokeke.'

'Are they still on that old quarrel?'

'Since they began it he has never been himself.'

'He has never been himself.' Chinwe spat and made a face. 'He has always been a devil.'

'O my chi!' After Chinwe had gone Nwamma contemplated the salt which she still carried on the wooden spoon. After a moment she seemed to arrive at a decision. She dipped the spoon into the pot, turned the soup. Then she lifted it up again and licked its back surface. The soup tasted as if it was done. She watched the pot for a spell then put it down and carried it into the grass hut. A little later, brushing off every sign of cooking she walked out of the compound. She went one by one to the three young men who were to come for the ozala and told them that Araba had a knife and that in his eyes there was murder.

A dangerous situation was thus avoided. But when the Uwadiegwus heard that Araba had once again defied their will they were furious. They held a tempestuous meeting and ostracized him. No Uwadiegwu was ever to enter his compound, no one was to gossip with his women, if he fell sick no one was to visit him.

'Stuttering!' shouted Araba as he got home. But his defiance lacked conviction. He knew how crushing the penalty could be. One may just as well be dead as be a social leper. Indeed he would have given in to them, except that it meant also accepting the man who had sought to take his life. Araba swore. He would get even with Nwokeke.

He had his consolation in the fact that Ani, goddess of the land, was taking note of Nwokeke's alus. For news came some days later that one of Nwokeke's wives had given birth to a baby girl. This was the eighth girl to be born to him. And one of his dearest wishes had always been to have a son. He had had to send away many of his wives who couldn't satisfy him in this direction; but the new ones with which he replaced them either didn't bear any children at all or had girls.

'It is the hand of Ani,' said Araba without malice.

'The eyes of Ani are not closed to the alus people make—'

'Yes,' said Okelekwu. In spite of the order forbidding members of the kindred to communicate with Araba, he visited him usually in the night. 'The eyes of ani are always open.'

'It is the way things happen. I know of some people who breathe alu out of their nostrils, speak alu with their mouths, look alu with their eyes. Do they think that Ani does not know?'

'No man can deceive the spirits for long,' said Okelekwu —But as the days went on the pressure of the umunna hatred began to tell. Friends no longer came to Araba to drink palm wine and in the evenings his large obi seemed very empty, assumed a funereal look.

But it was the wives who suffered most. Their best friends ignored them. And when they came to the common stream any Uwadiegwus that might be there turned their backs. The other wives bore the punishment meekly. With Chinwe it was different. She fought. One evening she came to the stream and walked defiantly into the midst of a chattering group of women. There was an uneasy, pregnant hush. One of the women, Okelekwu's wife, made a wry face and cocked a snook at her. But before she could complete the insult Chinwe caught her by her elbow and smacked her face hard. They fought savagely and at the end, tired and panting, their clay pots broken into pieces, their wrappers torn to shreds, they walked home, naked.

Under normal circumstances the Uwadiegwus could have called the two women up and punished them. But in this case to call Araba's wife up meant resuming contact with Araba and breaking his ostracism. Rather than do this the Uwadiegwus ignored the offence and the offenders.

Araba felt the humiliation keenly. He wouldn't have minded paying a fine but to be ignored rankled. For days he raved against Chinwe.

'But,'—

'Keep quiet!'

Chinwe stopped for a moment. Her eyes glowed with suppressed fury. A vein stood out on her neck. 'I will not keep quiet,' she said at last, unable to keep back her fury. 'You brought all the troubles on us. What do you want to do with an old ozala?'

Araba glared at her; but making a strong effort of will, he mastered his temper. That night when all the chickens had returned he went into Chinwe's hut and seized from an ogbu tree where the chickens had perched, a strong cock, the pride of Chinwe and of the roost. He carried it squawking powerfully into the obi and cut its throat and poured the blood on the Ikenga.

This was one of the tributes he exerted from wives who defied him.

But after the incident of the stream he knew it was futile trying to hold out against the combined will of the umunna. He began to make overtures to them. Okelekwu smoothed the way for him. A meeting was arranged at which Araba brought many pots of palm wine.

'That's how to go about it,' said Nwafo Ugo, eyeing the pots thirstily. 'As Danda would say, that which is in the pot should be in the belly.'

A few men laughed. They were in high spirits.

'Let's hear what he has to say,' said a gnarled grim-looking tapster.

'Kliklikli.'

'Yiii!'

'Kliklikli.'

'Yiii!'

'May each man have what is due to him. My voice is low. The proverb says that the word biko (please) never leads to a quarrel.'

'True! True!'

'If I have wronged you, my knees are on the ground. After all I am your son and a father doesn't bear ill-will against his own son for long.'

'No! No!'

'If a man cooks for the community, the community will eat it all. But if the community cooks for a single person he cannot eat the cooking.'

'Say no more!' roared the umunna, scrambling for their cups.

'You have come like a man,' said Nwafo Ugo.

The matter of the ofo was again shelved in the moment of thirst and reconciliation.

CHAPTER TWENTY

If Araba's illness had been fatal, Danda would have become the head of a large household of ten wives. He would have inherited a length of outer walls which would need to be covered regularly, and a long yam barn to be filled. As it was Araba lived at least for the mean time and Danda was free to take up his old life and, as Araba put it, to gad about in the manner agreeable to him and only to him and his chi.

One evening as he returned from a feast at Obunagu, Araba called him into the obi and asked him what he thought about marrying.

'It is sudden,' said Danda.

'It is not sudden. You are no longer young. It is time you had your own home.'

Araba had recently begun to feel anxious at not having grandsons. Most men of his age already had many. He had decided therefore that he would marry Danda to a wife. It would have been more impressive if Danda had been able to make the bride price for himself, but knowing Danda, Araba had little hope that he would.

Danda said that marriage was a good idea. 'We shall find a good woman, one with a full body and a fetching look. For you must admit that I myself have a full body and a face that women admire.'

Araba frowned. He had never thought much of height, being short himself, or of beauty which he considered womanly.

'What counts,' he said, 'is not how full your body is but what you can do with it.'

'True word,' laughed Danda.

To make up the money for the bride price, Araba had to sell some of his yams. The buyer who came the next day, Agbata Nnogu, was a shrewd farmer who looked as if he didn't eat enough but who was suspected of having a great deal of money put by somewhere.

Araba led him to the barn. They entered through a wicket door. Before them was an impressive sight. First, a long row of plump yam seeds strapped to standing posts which were joined together by lengths of raffia. Four such rows each about thirty yards long. Araba was in a way sorry that he had to sell them. The yam was a measure of a man's standing in the community. To diminish one's stock was like losing one of one's plumes. Then again the yam was nurtured by a man's sweat. It was a fruit of his blood. Therefore again it was part of him.

Agbata began at once.

'One row contains four hundred seedlings.'

'Five hundred.'

Agbata began to count. 'One has to be careful,' he said.

'Yes,' agreed Araba, disliking the other man a little.

'Twenty-five yams in twenty places,' murmured Agbata. His brow creased as he calculated. Squatting on his hams he made some marks on the ground.

'There are four hundred and five twenties,' said Araba.

'True,' said Agbata, 'but'—he rose with a worried face. 'You say each yam is a shilling?'

'That would give us twenty pounds and five.'

'Twenty and five!'

It took Agbata ten more minutes to arrive at this figure. 'Too much,' he said. 'Hai! Where do I get the money from. I have the fees of my children to pay. Ah! do you know, I nearly forgot about those fees. Sons of our fathers, I will not tell you a lie, all the money one earns nowadays goes into fees. And did you hear of my wife, she has fallen low with illness, the dibia we called in demands a goat. Don't you see, I am in trouble, I am a desperate man.'

Araba listened patiently and at the end said: 'Yams eat money nowadays. I cannot take off anything from twenty pounds and five.'

'Then there is tax. The world is hard—'

'Do you want to buy the yams or don't you?'

'It is well . . . Look, I shall pay you ten pounds.'

'Let us get out of here.'

'No, take it slow. We are not fighting.'

'Let us go.'

Agbata was no fool. He stopped pleading and changed the subject. 'They say there is smallpox in Mbammili.'

'Is there?'

'Yes,' Agbata snuffed. They were now seated on stools round one of the middle pillars in the obi. After a moment he rose and said: 'The sun is dying. I must go back home.'

'Stay well.'

'I greet you.'

The next day he returned and paid down twenty-two pounds. Araba took it without comment.

All the Uwadiegwus now combined to seek a wife for Danda. A find of Nwafo Ugo's was first considered.

'Her family is one of those who make noise at Eziakpaka,' he had said as a recommendation.

But on further investigation it turned out that somewhere in the past her family had been related to Araba's. That effectively ruled out any chances of marrying her. The next girl was from Obunagu and was said to be beautiful.

'Beauty costs money,' said Okelekwu.

'Yes, but should that stop us?' Nwafo winked in a way that was meant to be knowing. 'Every man likes to see beauty in his compound.'

'She has been to school, too, her parents say,' added the herdsman who had discovered her.

'No,' said Araba. 'We can't marry her.'

'Learning is all very well,' mused Nwafo Ugo. 'But it will be no good for Danda. He has never looked into a book since he was born.'

'And learning swells the bride price, we have to think of that,' concluded Okelekwu.

The kindred's choice finally fell on a girl from Mbammili. She hadn't been to a school. She was not beautiful though her looks were pleasant enough. Most important of all she was said to be a hard worker. Her parents were ready to marry her off, if they approved of her suitor.

Araba made sure that they did. On the day the go betweens from Mbammili came to his compound he feasted them well and made them costly presents. They were impressed and went home singing his praises.

The two families met two market weeks later in the plantain fringed compound of Udo of Mbammili, the girl's father. The host, a very old man, was surrounded by his kindred. He doddered up to meet Araba who also led a large crowd. The two parties exchanged praise names and compliments. Other rituals followed. Then Araba took upon himself the privilege of the first word.

He made quite a long job of it. At first he dealt with general things: the remembered history of Aniocha from which he, Araba, sprung; the fame of Mbammili from which the bride's father rose; the glorious past contrasting with these effeminate days; what qualities go to make a man; what qualities go to make a woman; how to treat a good woman; how to keep a bad one within bounds. Then it became specific; how manly the host, Udo, had shown himself; how he, Araba, looked forward to dealing with him. 'They call me Araba. Ask in Aniocha and they will tell you that that is a name to be reckoned with.'

'True word,' shouted the Uwadiegwus.

But Araba would say that the girl too came from a good home. The obi of her father was noised about.

Udo agreed firmly with the last sentiment and then went on to make a speech which matched his guest's in length and colour.

A period of snuff and low conversation followed. Then the bargaining started.

First an Mbammili hunch-back, whose style was poor, rose and said that the girl was pretty and should cost money. There was uneasy silence after that speech. Everybody had the feeling that there was something crude about it. The betrothal was a solemn ceremony that was subject to its own rules, possessed its own language. That phrase, for instance, 'cost money', was definitely bad form. So the hunch-back was ignored as being out of order.

Okelekwu rose next and made a speech tricked out with proverbs, tortuous, but through whose mazes some hints of money could be perceived. There was applause this time. That was more like it. The discussion had now been elevated to the high level of delicate, graceful parrying dear to the hearts of Ibo men. An equally eminent speaker from Mbammili performed next and seemed to suggest that a hundred pounds was not too much to ask for a pretty girl who was in addition a hard worker.

There was another spell of rumination. And then Araba stood and suggested his own price.

'Ten pounds!' shouted the hunch-back. '—Do you think you are buying a—'

'You are a fool, my friend!' roared Nwafo Ugo.

'I am—?'

'A stutterer!' The usually jovial Nwafo was amazingly transformed. His round good-natured cheeks became wobbly, his eyes, ordinarily twinkling with good humour, now flared up.

'Me a stutterer?' asked the hunch-back.

'Yes.'

'Call me a stutterer, would you? An akalogholi like you who cannot feed his family.'

It was inevitable that the quarrel must reach this stage where the opponents measured themselves against each other.

'Which one of us looks like a man, people of our land?' Nwafo appealed to the audience who, however, refused to take sides. 'Who looks well-fed and who looks hungry? Whose arms are a man's?'

'I will haul you out of here!' shrilled the plucky hunch-back. 'Come to my compound and see my yam-barn. Come and let me feed you.'

'You merely fell the iroko with your tongue. Feed yourself first. Feed yourself and feed your starving family. Akalogholi!'

The quarrel was quenched by the collective voice of the people.

The combatants sat back, the hunch-back's small eyes

boring into his opponent's with venom. Nwafo's countenance twitching back fiercely. They were at it for a minute
and then Nwafo, recovering his good-humour first, turned to
a friend nearby and laughed.

Danda restored the original mood of ease with one of his
speeches. He had seen the girl, he said. True she wasn't big,
she wouldn't measure up to him. 'I am a full-bodied man.'
But if she would behave and call him master he was
ready to have her.

There was much flowery talk after this. But agreement
was arrived at somehow. The girl's parents at first stood at
seventy pounds. Araba and his followers crept up to fifty
but later paid down fifty-five which proved acceptable.
The palaver dragged on through reminiscences and finally
ended on the brink of night. The guests, full of palm wine
and animated all the way by Danda's flute, staggered home
with the moon.

CHAPTER TWENTY-ONE

The coming out or marriage celebration took place in the
market some weeks later. A large crowd from the ten towns
attended. From morning till noon laughing, gaily-dressed
dancers, musical bands, fluters came into Aniocha market;
Danda's numerous friends, acquaintances, minstrels from
the hill villages, raffish masqueraders from the wet valleys,
rascals, hardy loafers, men of doubtful reputation, all the
motley crew with which Danda had knocked about in his
picaresque career rallied to see him marry.

The reverberation of the drums mingled and the dancers
clashed. The noise was deafening. And it even swelled
when Danda came in, dressed in bells and cloak, borne on
the shoulders of Nnoli Nwego.

'Oi! Oi! Oi! My father bore me well. My chi created me
well.' This assertion was loudly cheered.

Danda's wife was borne in from Mbammili. She was carefully prettified. She had on new ear-rings and a colourful wrapper. Her skin glowed with camwood. She looked very small and was scarcely seen above the heads of the men on whose shoulders she sat. But those who saw her remarked her pretty face and her large, intense eyes which all the time she was on view were fixed unwaveringly on her husband.

'My father begot me well. My chi created—' Danda's excitement overwhelmed him. He escaped from the arms of his bearer, jumped down and began to flute. The crowd rejoiced. Their exultation even drowned the noise of the drums.

It lasted for an hour or so. Then everybody began to move away.

The wind was fading away silently. The ogbu trees in the market had begun to brood. It looked as if every living thing was hurrying home. The sun had sunk but had spread over the door through which he went five flaming fingers that seemed to bid farewell.

'My chi created me well—' The assertion drifted away and received little sympathy, for the market was almost empty. The musicians had taken the wife home and snatches of their music came from a distance as if from another world. The palm roofed stalls were now beginning to shrink.

'My father begot me well.' Danda had made his last splash in Aniocha and all was silence.

'Our day is ended,' said Nnoli. He and Okoli Mbe had waited until the end. They sat on the ogwe drinking from the only calabash which had been forgotten by the other celebrants.

Danda sat between them. Every now and then he would shout 'oi! oi! oi!' He was very drunk.

Some time passed and gradually the world was covered with flimsy darkness. Through it a figure groped its way in the darkness.

'Who says it is he?' asked Okoli Mbe.

'Danda!' a voice cried. 'Araba says that we await you.'

'We shall come when the world has righted. Have some palm wine.'

The messenger groped for the cup, drank and went away.

The night now became darker and there was a great void all around as when the black soup pot is emptied of bitter-leaf soup and covered with a broken potsherd and is left in the corner to wait for the night when it might be made alive again.

A second message was soon brought: 'Should Araba marry for Danda and also help him to go in to his wife?'

'The day has broken its legs,' said Danda rising. His friends stood up too, and sang him away. At the point where the approaches to Araba's compound branched off from the main road. Danda left them. They stood at the junction bawling into the night.

'Danda is gone. The mellow flute, the ogene voice is no more. The bright masquerade that flamed like ripe palm nuts has left us.'

Meanwhile the bright masquerade was being led to his room where his wife was waiting. And when he reached it Araba and Okelekwu pushed him in and locked the door.

CHAPTER TWENTY-TWO

We were all anxious to know how the new couple got on. The first news was favourable. It was said that they were a well-matched pair. But this news was contradicted by a report which came to us a few days later.

They say that two market weeks after the marriage celebrations Danda went to his father-in-law at Mbammili and demanded his bride price back. But (as the story would have it) Araba went after him and countered the request by claiming that the bride price was his not Danda's. They tell how Danda had been aroused and how father and son had nearly come to blows. Udo, the father-in-law, had made peace between them. Then he had advised Danda to suffer his wife a little more patiently and to remember what the bed-bug had said to his children: 'Take heart, what is now hot will some day become cold.'

For some time after this we heard nothing more.

But then one fine morning Danda was seen, hoe on shoulder, long basket on head, walking to the farm. He had taken off his belled cloak and it was a little difficult to recognize him without it. Knots of curious spectators standing tip-toe at the outer walls of their compound watched him pass and commented:

'She must have used ogwu on him.'

'Then the ogwu must be in those eyes. I have never seen eyes like those before.'

'Stuttering,' said Chinwe, when that evening she was told of the new gossip. She had assumed the position of mentor to Danda's wife since she came into the obi, helped her in setting up her own home and warned her against 'our big head'. That day two of them, carrying heavy pots on their heads, were returning from the stream when they heard some men behind them mention Danda's name. Chinwe, raising her voice so that those men might hear, said:

'Of course a wife cannot be expected to allow her husband always to gad about like a scamp.'

There was little gadding about indeed in the months that lay ahead, for work on the farm was heavy and Danda's hands were full. His absence was more and more remarked in the few celebrations held in the neighbouring villages. Often when people from those places saw an Aniocha man they would ask him:

'How is Rain?'

And the Aniocha man would say: 'Rain now has work in hand.'

At Aniocha he drank less palm wine and talked less. When he came to the ogwe in the evening it was not to shout 'Hoa! God created the world!' but to complain about the heavy rains or about the damage the crickets were doing to the farms. His most popular witticism was no longer: 'That which is in the pot should be in the belly,' but: 'Women are fire coals which a man open-eyedly heaps on his head.'

'The day has opened,' said Araba delightedly.

'I thought he would be a new man,' said Okelekwu. 'You remember that time you complained of him. I told you that he might change. A wife was all he needed. When I was in Agidi—'

'He has changed,' said Araba. 'And all will be well.'

And all might have been well after this. Danda might have settled down and become a good man. There is no knowing.

But in fact what happened was this: one day he disappeared from home. We searched for him in vain. All sorts of rumours began to circulate. But three days after that, he came back, very drunk.

His wife acting on the advice of Chinwe refused to give him any food for a full day. Danda retorted by calling up the Onyekulie.

You have perhaps heard of this scurrilous-tongued guardian of manhood. His place among the great ones of Aniocha was peculiar and never very high. He appeared on earth as a rascally gnome and helped husbands to keep restless women within bounds. In the middle of the night he would emerge from the unholy bush, dressed in plantain leaves, braying in an eerie voice. For hours he stood by the hut of the refractory woman and called her names. She would be so terrified that she would beg her husband to call the spirit off. The next day she cooked him cocoyam with vegetables or any other delicacy; and domestic harmony would be restored.

The Onyekulie had never been known to fail. So when that night his voice was heard near the Araba compound all the women trembled.

'Who is it for?' murmured Chinwe. 'What have we done to the devil?'

Araba had often accused Chinwe of being unfaithful and called up the Onyekulie for her. Neither were his suspicions entirely baseless. Few of the wives of multi-wived obis could do without having a lover or two on the sly.

But Chinwe needn't have worried. For this particular Onyekulie did not address her but Danda's new wife.

'Nwadu, wife of Rain, the story has been told that you do not feed your husband. Why? Do you want to kill him? You want to take a lover? Tell me the truth? Go on, confess. Is it true that you have been smiling at Nwoyeoka the tree-cutter? Yes . . . We smell evil. We live in the land of the spirits but we see all that is done in the land of men. Nwadu, wife of Danda—'

Danda himself stood at the door of the gate, looking out at his spirit allies and waiting for his wife to come and submit. Not long after her name had been called she came, all in a tremble.

'Ask him to go away.'

'Eh?'

'Send him away.'

'It is well.' Danda called out to the Onyekulie. 'Spirit of our fathers, it is enough. Spare her.'

And the fat Onyekulie waddled away back to the land of the spirits.

Early the next morning Danda sat in his hut and waited for the cocoyam and vegetables with which Nwadu was to reward him for his coming to her succour the previous night.

But instead of the customary delicacy Nwadu brought a colourless breakfast of roasted yam and palm oil.

'You have no cocoyam in your house?'

'No.' All the fear of yesterday had left her and now she appeared in a happy morning mood. Her small pretty face had a lot of colour. 'Why did you call up the Onyekulie?' she asked. 'Have I ever done anything to you?'

'You have spoken alu, woman. Nobody calls up the Onyekulie. It comes from the land of spirits by itself.'

'Land of spirits!' Nwadu laughed gleefully. 'You will tell me, too, that it was not Nnoli Nwego's voice I heard last night.'

'Double alu!'

A few hours later Nnoli and a friend sat on the ogwe by the motor station discussing the matter.

'They tell me that Rain's wife has told the secret of the masquerade,' Nnoli said.

'What!' shouted the man, jumping down from the second tier of the ogwe and nearly injuring himself. 'Who?'

'Danda's wife. She said that the Onyekulie was only a man.'

'But why do you tell me?' The man's face shrank with fear. 'Why do you fill my ear with the story? Have I ever done any harm to you?'

'There is nothing to fear.'

'I didn't hear a thing. I wasn't listening.' And trembling, the man made his escape.

Araba was furious when he heard the story.

'They will ruin me!' he shouted at Okelekwu as if the latter was one of them.

'Telling the secret of the masquerade is not a small thing,' agreed Okelekwu waving his whisk. 'A man eats sand for it.'

'Anyway, she is Danda's wife and he will have to answer to Aniocha. I am not in it,' said Araba bitterly.

But in spite of this he called Nwadu. She answered the call from Chinwe's hut.

'It is Chinwe who has been teaching her tricks,' said Araba to Okelekwu.

Nwadu came, dressed in two butterfly-blue wrappers one of which was tied above her breast while the other belted her in the middle. Araba observed her keenly. He hadn't seen much of her since her marriage. And now that she was before him he was surprised at how short she was. But there was no doubt that she was pretty. He could appreciate this.

'Sit down,' he said. He would not be harsh with her. She was young and a newcomer to the obi.

She sat down on a round stool. Outwardly she was calm but at heart she was a little overwhelmed. She had not expected that a sentence she had made in a moment of levity would cause so much trouble.

Araba had been thinking of a way of beginning, a way that would reassure her and at the same time make it clear to her how grave her alu was. At last he began.

'You have made an alu. A powerful alu. In the days gone

by—well, that would have been the end of everything, but now the ozos will only carry your husband.' He paused.

Okelekwu nodded assent.

'There are quarrels in all houses,' he went on, 'but the husband and wife don't come out and spread them to the whole people.' He paused again to see what she had to say. But she continued to gaze on the floor.

'You have nothing to say?' he asked a little sharply.

She looked up and said the first thing that came into her head:

'A wife cannot be expected to allow her husband always to gad about like a scamp.'

'So?' said Araba with a formidable stare. 'Your husband is a scamp?'

But perhaps what Araba objected to in the speech was not so much that it was disrespectful to Danda as that it implied contempt for the Araba obi. To call the first son of the compound a scamp was as bad an insult as could possibly be.

Nwadu was again thrown into confusion. She had only repeated Chinwe's words and hadn't had time to weigh them and prune out some that might carry nasty undertones.

'You do not know how lucky you are to be married into this obi. Your father, Udo, who is my friend, has a big obi but he would have told you that it is not to be compared to the one in which you sit. I will hush up your alu because the Araba name makes noise in Aniocha. But you must beware.'

'It is well.' She was a little relieved to have got off so cheaply.

'That's it.'

She rose and went.

Danda came in a few minutes later. His face was grim and a little worried. He had put off his cloak and now wore a rough army woollen shirt over his loin cloth.

'They tell me that your wife has brought big trouble on our heads,' Araba said by way of conversation.

Danda kept a sullen silence. He was looking for the pot

of palm wine. He found it at last but it was empty. Hissing with disappointment he came up to where Okelekwu sat and took his own seat.

'The beginning of anything is always hard,' said Okelekwu sympathetically, 'but with patience everything will be well.'

'I will send her home,' Danda burst out.

'That's not the way to go about it,' said Okelekwu. 'One doesn't send one's wife home just because one is angry with her. I have lived with my second wife for some ten years and there is hardly a single day that I don't hear a hard word from her. But I don't send her home. If every man is allowed to send his wife home at the first sign of difficulty there will be no marriages left.'

'I will send her home.'

'Do,' said Araba calmly. 'But get me my bride price first. Go to Udo and snatch back our money.'

'He won't give it back,' said Okelekwu with conviction. 'I know Udo.'

'An akalogholi,' said Araba. 'But an obstinate one.'

'I will get the money from him,' said Danda.

Araba snuffed and shook the calves of his legs happily. He did not believe a word of what Danda said.

Danda later found he couldn't send Nwadu home. For she was found to be pregnant. And everybody now honoured her.

CHAPTER TWENTY-THREE

The scorch season had come round again. The kite had returned and had been hovering around the countryside looking for chickens. Work had lessened. Feast days had increased and now men and women could laugh with all their teeth.

For many days Danda had been knocking up the neighbours warning them that the time had come. They would dress and hasten to the Araba compound. But there they found Nwadu blithely going about her household chores.

'Hai,' one woman complained. 'Have we ever heard of such a childbirth. I dare say the birth of a child to the King of the oibo [white] land would not be so noised about.'

'Let him make noise,' replied another woman. 'I don't blame him. The first child is very sweet.'

Danda made noise. Especially when the baby came. They first brought it to him.

'Welcome,' he said, holding it gingerly. 'You have come to a big obi.'

'Slow, slow!' some women who were about said.

'I won't harm him,' said Danda. 'When the mother-hen steps on one of her chicks she doesn't harm it.'

After that he wrapped himself well with his blue cloak, polished the bells, took his flute and tinkled to market.

'People of my land, it is a man,' he announced to the world. 'A tax payer.'

'Well done, Danda,' they said, shaking hands. 'You have been a man.'

'Every one of you must come to my house and drink with me. I don't say I am rich. I am a poor man, but what I have I give you. And even if I have nothing but the air, you will still come and show me your smiling faces. If there is a man here to whom what is good is not good let him come out.'

'There is no such person!' roared the crowd.

'Give us palm wine.' He accepted a cup from a well-wisher and drank and jingled to another group of people.

'It is a man,' he informed them. 'They say he has my face, people of my land. He hasn't only my face, my hands my feet. He is me, another Danda.'

'Welcome, Danda. There is a man in you.'

'Oi! Oi! Oi! God created the world.' Danda danced an ogwulugwu step. 'The day is complete,' he said.

And when he came home that evening he was still holding forth. 'He is going to be a great man in our kindred,' he assured the people who sat in the obi.

'Ahai! So we already know what his future will be!' laughed Nwafo.

'Yes,' Danda said with conviction. 'I have spoilt my life,' he added happily, 'but he won't spoil his. He will reach where they say people reach. If going to oibo land is the newest thing then he will go there and come back and be noised about.'

Danda sipped palm wine. 'Hoa! that which is in the pot should be in the belly.'

Araba was no less pleased. His hard leathery face was often seen to crinkle and his mouth to twitch in what very much resembled a smile. Once again he kept an open house to the kindred. When they gathered in the obi he sat in their midst and laid down the law.

He supervised the nursing of the baby too. The youngest daughter of Chinwe used to carry him about. Often as she passed by she would be tossing him recklessly up and catching him again. Sometimes she would slip and the baby would be in danger of toppling down. Araba who all the while had been watching would shout:

'Is that how to carry a baby?'

And sometimes the baby would wake up in the middle of the night crying. Araba, who slept very lightly, would rise, walk up to the wall of Nwadu's hut and speak over it.

'Don't you know how to take care of a baby?'

And when the baby was a few months old, Araba used to ask the mother on certain evenings to bring 'our man'. She would bring him.

Araba would lay him on his hairy chest. The baby would feel the pricks of the white hair and protest. Then Araba would lay him on a goat-skin spread on the ojo and begin to talk to him.

'Ikem Araba' (Ikem Danda would have been more appropriate).

'Don't give me that one. I know you. You are a clever one!'

The baby replied with a 'boo!' fixing his large liquid eyes on his grandfather's small bloodshot ones and probably wondering how a human being could get so old.

'Don't take after your father. He is no good. Be worthy of our obi. He smiles. What is it that is amusing you?'

He would go on in this strain until the baby fell asleep, then he would gently raise him to his shoulder. And there he stayed until his mother came for him.

CHAPTER TWENTY-FOUR

'The question is: how will the ozo anklet look on Danda?' bawled Nwora Otankpa.

'How do you mean? There are some people on whom the anklets frown?' said Okelekwu.

'That's not what I mean. One can never be sure what Danda will do the next moment.'

Two of them and a few other men sat under a huge ube tree which shaded the greater part of Okelekwu's small, cosy compound. Okelekwu had just sent for cola and as the oldest of those present was breaking it, Nwora returned to the subject of their talk.

'Listen to me,' he said. 'I don't say Araba is not wealthy. He is twice as wealthy as we but he can't take the ozo title twice.'

'He said he would.'

In my knowledge there has been only one other Aniocha man who has taken the ozo title twice. Ejiofo Omile. And he had a barn that would have fed the whole of Aniocha. Araba couldn't measure up to him.'

'He said he would take it,' asserted Okelekwu a little annoyed by Nwora's doggedness. 'I heard it with these two ears of mine. I don't care what ozo Ejiofo was like. Araba said to the ozos that he would take the title for Danda. And I know he will.'

'Araba likes big talk.'

'You haven't been to his house lately.'

In Araba's house there was noise and bustle, much going to and fro. The obi and all the eleven huts of the women swarmed with strangers. There were relatives from the ten towns. Then there were friends from other lands. These last made a great impression wherever they went. They spoke the Ibo tongue with a refreshing breadth of accent and Aniocha wags found a new pleasure in mimicking them. Their women wore strange hair styles and flashy ornaments: copper bells and bangles that sang and tinkled all over the compound.

Every few moments a huge load of firewood was carted in by noisy, sweaty men. Two black shorthorn cows of the breed known as 'Ibo cow,' to distinguish it from the lighter-coloured, larger, thinner variety which the Hausas bring down from the North, stood tied to the orange tree in the middle of the compound. Behind the obi and between it and the long wall which separated the women's huts from the main yard a huge pile of firewood lay. Nnoli Nwego was busy breaking some of it, gasping and spitting sweat. Some women were passing by and stood to watch him.

'It is the only type of job his eyes light up for,' said Chinwe, referring to Nnoli's preference for breaking wood only in those houses where a feast is preparing.

'I know what type of job your eyes light up for,' said Nwafo, glad to use this repartee as an excuse for a short rest. His muscles which had been stretched by labour regained their bulge. Chinwe stared at them and a warm light came into her eyes.

'Araba hasn't two mouths,' Okelekwu said. 'His yes is yes.'

Soon, even sceptics were congratulating him. Araba accepted the homage with dignity. There had only been one other ozo who had bought the title for his son. Ejiofo Omile. And his name lived in proverbs. Araba's would too. Already the praise singers and trumpeters were vying with each other to invent superlatives for him.

To deserve these had not been easy. The ozo takes away all the strength from a man. Cases have been known of some men who after buying it have had to go through life ruined even though retaining the honour of the name. Araba knew too that buying the title might break him.

A greater part of his yams had been sold. Relatives had lent some money which would have to be repaid and even then the sum of £200 which was calculated to cover all the expense was not yet made up. Still Araba awaited the future with calm.

Danda enjoyed the present. The scorch season was at the height of its splendour and he was much in demand in various places. But he didn't go anywhere, he was giving a feast himself. His cloak was dyed purple in princely fashion with camwood, he had already begun to wear the anklets of rank. He carried his own ngwu agelega made in his own forge. He had put on weight and his eyes had a very attractive sparkle. People remarked that he was getting younger.

There were three candidates for the ozo rank this year. There had originally been only two. Araba had informed the ozos too late of his intention to make Danda the third. When he did, many insisted that he postpone his title-taking until the next scorch season. No, Araba persisted. At last the ozos, unable to resist his will and in any case never too unwilling to admit into their club those who could pay, reluctantly gave in.

Every evening the other two candidates walked the roads preceded by their praise singers who blew the candidates' names to with ozalas. Whenever they came by Araba's compound they would call out in round syllables.

'Danda, nwa amul n'ego ekenemuo!' ('Danda, son born in money, I greet you.')

'Nwa mulu n'aku ekenemuo.'

Danda, his bells jingling, leapt out and before a delighted audience would dance with his fellow aristocrats. Then they would go round the town fluting and singing.

Already the first of the ceremonies that preceded the ozo had been concluded. A day is usually set out when the people who are to take the ozo have the right to go into the farm of any Aniocha man and if they see any ripe palm fruit or coconuts cut them and take them away. Danda and his followers had been able to gather rich prizes.

One man, however, they couldn't outwit. Ebenebe had hired many labourers to prevent his being robbed. From the first cry of the cocks they waited by his palms and coconut trees. As soon as it was dawn they climbed them and quickly saved the prizes.

The next ceremony was going to be of greater moment. The invitation to all ozo men to a preliminary feast during which they officially approved the new ozo's candidature. They came early to Araba's compound. Aniocha men, as Nwafo Ugo would say, were always punctual to feasts.

'Call them to work,' says Nwafo, 'and on that day they would first go to their farms—"to repair a little thing"— and would need a messenger to come and remind them. Call them to a feast and they would start very early to watch the sun, every now and then saying to their wives: "Is it time?"'

Idengeli was the first to come, and brought the cheering news that he would give Araba two goats as his own contribution to the ozo expenses.

'You have worked like a man,' said Araba.

'No, it is you who have worked like a man.'

The ozos had now all come. They began with the baskets of baked cassava. When these were done they went on with the plain wine. Now was the time for compliments, for the ozos to stand and praise their host. The first person to rise was Nwora Otankpa who had entered the ozo only last scorch season.

'Kliklikli.'

'Yiii.'

'Kliklikli.'

'Yiii.'

'Some people see the truth and turn away their eyes. And because of this things continue to spoil.'

Some ozos jerked to attention at this dramatic opening. A few, however, were sceptical. The young man would have his drama.

'True word!' roared Nwora. 'When things go the wrong way somebody should have the courage to arrest them.

I am not afraid of anyone,' he bristled at Araba, 'I come from a great obi myself; anybody who denies this let him come out.' He threw the challenge with a violent gesture.

The ozos began to murmur impatiently.

But Nwora would not reveal himself yet. He went on cocooning his mystery. But after some time he began to unwind the strands.

'Did any of you see me touch a speck of cassava this evening? No. But the rest of you sucked your fingers, drank palm wine and rejoiced. Go on then but don't ask me to join you until you have proved to me that the laws of our fathers should be thrown to the dust.'

'Hai!' He lowered his head and hunched his shoulders like an aggressive bull. His cowtail moustaches stiffened.

'What do the laws of our fathers say? Tell me what do those laws say? A man who runs away from the ici cannot be taken into the ozo. Didn't Danda once run away from the ici?' Nwora ended as dramatically as he had begun and sat down with an expression of disgust.

It seemed such a little thing but there was no getting round it. Araba's closest friends had nothing to say. Idengeli shook his head sadly.

A little thing, perhaps; but Ojadili went to the land of the spirits, wrestled with spirit-heroes and conquered, but when he returned to the land of men he died of the bite of a housefly.

Such a small thing. But Nwokeke's last and most successful checkmate.

'A small point like that,' mused Okelekwu, waving his whisk after the ozos had all gone.

'It is true,' said Araba. 'And that was why I nearly killed him.'

'Who?'

'Danda,' Araba brought his face grimly close to Okelekwu's. Okelekwu tapped himself with the cowtail whisk as if brushing away evil.

'He was a boy then. I had a quarrel with Onyeocha Agali and you know how it is, you raise your voice when you are angry. Two of us spoke up about our sons. Onyeocha had a son; he is now dead; but at that time he was ill and a weakling. Still his father said to me that he was more a man than Danda. I laughed.'

'Hold that baby well.' This was directed at the small girl who was passing by throwing Danda's son about.

'I laughed. But four days afterwards the boys of Danda's age were to cut the ici. Onyeocha's son was one of them and he bore the pain without a murmur. But Danda, where was Danda? He had run away and my face was washed with shame. Two weeks later he returned. And I took the akalogholi by the throat and kicked him into the pit of death and locked it.'

'Ahai!' cried Okelekwu ruffled out of his habitual sadness.

'Yes,' Araba pressed one of his fingers on the left nostril, sneezed through the other and with his right leg spread the sputum on the floor.

'I had had enough of him. And that would have been his end. But he came out, I don't know how. Nwamma must have done something to the pit of death.'

'And so all these things we had bought—'

But Danda's bells announced him and in a short moment he came in. He was in a state of haste and the chatter of his bells was a little incoherent. He put his left foot on the ojo and standing half in, half out, said:

'Where are the ozos?'

'Come in here,' said Araba.

Danda, a little puzzled, came in and sat down on one of the stools.

'A friend at Uruoji made a feast for me and we were singing there. Haven't the ozos come yet? They are late.'

'They have gone,' said Araba calmly.

'How? Gone?'

'There will be no ozo title for you. The law says that a man who has once run away from the ici cannot enter into the ozo. And this evening Nwora Otankpa reminded the ozo men that you once ran away from the ici.'

'Nwora Otankpa?' Danda seized on this name. 'The fool!

145

I knew it was he. It couldn't be anybody else. I will deal with him some day. His father has no ici. There must be many people in Aniocha who have not cut the ici.'

'That is not the point. The point is that there will be no ozo for you.'

'There will be,' asserted Danda. 'If the ozos bind their heads with akwala string we will have the title without them. They don't know who they have to deal with. Give us palm wine.'

'Prepare to have your face cut.'

'How is that?'

'Day after tomorrow.'

'But—'

'I will go now to Eziakpaka and call the ogbu ici. Day after tomorrow he will work on your face. It will take no more than four market weeks to heal. Then we will call the ozos again.'

'It is well, but—'

Araba rose, slung his goatskin bag over his shoulder and, followed by Okelekwu, walked out.

CHAPTER TWENTY-FIVE

It was the night before Danda was to cut the ici. The prospects of the ordeal did not seem to have affected his spirits. He stood full-blown in the middle of the compound talking to a crowd and laughing. There was a young moon and its soft light gave Danda's blue cloak a satiny hue. His bells, polished for the occasion, twinkled like fireflies.

'That's how it is, people of your land.' And Danda began to sing.

As soon as the first notes of the oja were heard outside the compound a crowd gathered—men, women, children jostled into Araba's compound to hear Danda sing his last song in Aniocha. He sang with the flute but it was easy for most people in the audience to translate the notes into words, they had heard the song many times before:

'I have been everywhere. Remember when we were at Mbaukwu which is as red as camwood. Where are you, Okoyeocha, my friend? My voice is ringing for you.

'Hai. Another animal climbs with the monkey and breaks its neck. Where is Okoyeocha. Come and ring my hand or my tone will dry.

'They said to me, sing. I sang of the hunter who misses the first ndulu. Let him not bite his lips for another will come, I said. And of the child who carries fire and carries a knife. If the fire does not burn him the knife will cut him. And of the spear thrown at an antheap? It will either break or bend I told them.

'Kokoya! I sang to them. I said do not complain that soup has entered in your eyes when you are inside a stream. The snake climbs the top of the iroko tree. Without hand or feet but with his chi. You have your chi.

'Kokoya! They said to me, sing. I sang to them. Men of the land of alulani. They threw nsi at me. I said to them, why do you throw nsi at me. If what is good is not good to you then let your wives give birth to crocodiles and let's see how you will like it.

'Kokoya! Spare the flower and the ododo. The ododo is meant to be admired. It's not meant to be used for a burial. Why do you keep the wine in the pot? That which is in the pot should be in the belly. And no colour of camwood can colour night into day.

'So let's get home to the land of our fathers. The day is closing in upon us. The sun is footsore and has gone to sleep. When things go hard with the poor man he calls his kindred.

'So we returned to the mkpuke of our mothers. And the land broke its legs and became a ravine. And our voice became dry.'

As soon as he finished there was a chorus of cheering. Many coins were thrown at him by admirers but he ignored them. Okoli Mbe, smiling shrewdly, gathered the coins and tied them in a loop at the edge of his wrapper.

After a moment Nnoli Nwego broke out into his own

song in a sepulchral voice which caused laughter and some ironic cheers.

'Go it, son of our fathers!'

'That's how it is, men of our lands.' Danda took over from him. 'The children are hungry. Let their mothers return from the market and give them food.'

CHAPTER TWENTY-SIX

'It is too late,' said Nwafo Ugo.

'They won't succeed,' Nwora Otankpa cut in.

'Why shouldn't they succeed?' said Nwokeke Idemmili rubbing his extensive stomach tenderly.

'True,' mused Okelekwu, waving his whisk. 'It is better to have the ici when one is young. But there is no harm in cutting it later. The skin of the older man is tough but he is also stronger and can bear it better.'

'I have never seen anyone of Danda's age cutting the ici,' said Nwafo. 'Whatever concerns Danda is different.'

There was laughter. Nwafo rubbed his bottom with the pride of a wit.

The morning had just awakened from sleep, throwing off its cold blue wrapper and yawning. More and more men were drifting into the Araba compound to watch the ici. Some had brought their own stools, others cowhides. Those who had neither stool nor cowhide sliced off leaves of the plantain, spread them on the ground and sat on them.

They waited.

Suddenly there broke through the air the song of ngwele kwonwu. This strange bird got its name from what it seems to say: ngwele kwonwu—kwonwu—kwonwu—kwonwu (lizard there is death—death—death).

A most accurate augurer of death; whenever it whistles its mournful tale men shiver.

'Who has died?' asked Nwafo Ugo.

'I haven't heard,' sighed Okelekwu.

Nwafo made a sign round his head to ward off the evil. 'I wonder what Danda's face will look like after the ici.'

'Not very bright!' roared Nwora Otankpa. 'I remember my own days. The ici stings like pepper.'

'If Danda is lucky he will come off without shame. He has no enemies.'

The great point of the ici is that it is a test of fortitude. The ogbu ici rips off pelts of flesh in a traditional pattern that stretches from ear to ear. The operation is excruciating. But the victim is to bear the pain if not with a smile at least without any visible show of sorrow. If he winces or cries out, he breaks the magic of the ritual and lets down himself and his kindred.

The enemies of the man whose face is being cut often take advantage of this weakness. With the aid of a strong ogwu they transform themselves into scorpions or red-ants, creep under the victim, bite or sting him and make him cry out and thereby earn the worst of shames.

'No nsi can harm Danda,' said Okelekwu. 'Araba's hand is strong. He has power.'

Strong charms hung on bamboo posts at the four corners of the compound. Then four family gods stood guard by the bed on which the ici ceremony was to be performed.

Araba and Danda sat in the obi. Between them were the rest of the family gods and a pot of palm wine topped by a gourd cup.

'So all our load is on your shoulder,' Araba was whispering. 'Our name is here and the world is there. What am I saying? Do you want palm wine?'

'Yes.'

Araba's hands trembled as he gave Danda the gourd cup.

'When I cut my own ici, my eyelids did not flicker. And the whole of Aniocha marvelled. They say that my father, Udeji Uwadiegwu, took his own with a heart of stone. He was a strong man. I have never yet seen a stronger. You still want more palm wine?'

'Yes.'

Araba served him absentmindedly, still observing the past.

Danda drank thirstily and stretched his hand for more.

'Quite true,' said Araba, at last waking up from his reverie. Then he said with a firm tone:

'You must do it.'

'I will do it.'

'The eyes of our fathers are open.'

Danda next went to speak to his mother.

'Are you hungry?' Outwardly she was calm.

'What have you got?'

She scooped into a wooden plate Danda's favourite food —breadfruit mixed with maize—and passed it to him. As he ate she watched him fixedly. She would rather there were no ici. She had seen Nwaku Eke's son cut his own ici. When they finished with him he looked dead. They crammed into his unconscious mouth various delicacies. Praise singers sang and gun shots were let off. There was glory in the ici but the penalty for failure—

Danda had finished the breadfruit.

'You want more?' she asked.

'Yes.'

She filled the plate again. And Danda once again cleaned it out. Before he went she asked him:

'You will do it?'

'Yes, I will.'

'The eyes of our fathers are open.'

The ogbu ici had just come. A lean hawk of a fellow with a sharp manner and twinkling eyes. As Danda came up to him he sharpened his knife on his palm, and beamed. His manner was reassuring. It seemed to suggest: 'Come along, don't be afraid, I will kill you with only one stroke.'

The bed was the type made of raffia and standing on four legs cut out of the branches of the akpaka tree. It was covered with a flowered piece of cloth and at its head was a bundle of clothes that would serve as a pillow.

Gingerly Danda lay flat on the bed and stared at the ogbu

ici's knife which glinted with the morning sun.

'Close your eyes, Danda,' said Okelekwu.

'No,' said Nwafo. 'Let him see. Ndulu the bird says that the gun he sees cannot kill him.'

This sally was greeted with laughter. The men were in high spirits.

The ogbu ici first washed Danda's face with a soft cloth soaked in sweet-smelling ointment. Then he cut two almost parallel lines near the right eye and began to remove the pelt of skin between them.

There were some of the men around who were still squeamish about blood and involuntarily closed their eyes. But even those who were attentive could not be sure what really went wrong.

There were a few who hadn't time to get out of the way. They only felt a sensation of a body leaping over their heads. Some blood had dropped on the right hand of Nwafo Ugo. He rose and went to clean it on the body of the orange tree nearby.

For a long time the ogbu ici held that sharp knife as if he wasn't quite sure what to do with it. Finally he sighed, dropped it and went out.

Araba walked firmly into his obi, sat down before the Ikenga and began to murmur something.

'Well, what are we waiting for?' asked Nwokeke, smiling at the stupefied kindred.

The tension broke and there were murmurs of small talk as the people beat dust off their cowhides and began to disperse. Okelekwu looked curiously at Araba, felt like going in to sit by him, decided against doing so and walked home alone, caressing the air with his whisk.

'The sun is awake,' said Nwokeke to Nwora Otankpa.

'Yes,' agreed the latter, looking at the great daub of colour which took up the whole of the eastern sky. 'Today will be fine. I will go to my valley farm.'

They moved out and soon arrived at a huge akpaka tree on the side of the road. They sheltered in its shade for a long time and at last walked on still talking.

A small bird with black and dirty-copper feathers had
sat directly above their heads preening his wings. And as
soon as they left he stretched, yawned and flew off chanting
tauntingly : ngwele kwonwu—kwonwu—kwonwu.

CHAPTER TWENTY-SEVEN

It was one of those rare mornings of the scorch season,
cool and light. A faint bluish mist was coming down from
the sky and settling on the sandy ebe. There was a salty
tang in the air which probably blew from the yams that
were being roasted in the nearby fields.

A small knot of men squatted, sat, stood on the ebe. They
had come to solemnize the death of Araba. Nwokeke presided. Others present included Idengeli, and Akumma Nwego.
Nwafo Ugo carried a drum slung over his left shoulder.
Okelekwu was missing.

All Aniocha had been invited but many of the other clans
had declined the invitation. They complained that the
messengers who had been sent to them had not brought the
customary cola—two pots of palm wine. But one couldn't
help wondering if they wouldn't indeed have overlooked
the oversight if they had known that there would be a great
deal of palm wine in Araba's obi.

Of the Uwadiegwus themselves only a few came. The
Christians among them had been forbidden to attend. A
new order had been made against churchmen who attended
pagan rituals or took part in them, who were seen dancing
on pagan feast days, singing pagan songs or carrying pagan
masquerades. Such people would on their death not receive
Christian burial. This dire threat decided the flexible-con-
scienced converts who had enjoyed the best of both reli-
gions. They were now to choose between heaven and the
church, on the one hand, hell and paganism on the other.

'Where are the drummers?' said Idengeli. 'We cannot wait
here for ever.'

'Okelekwu has gone for them,' said Nwafo. 'I couldn't find anybody to come with me so Okelekwu said he would try.' Nwafo beat a tattoo on a drum which was slung across his shoulder.

'No drummers in the whole of Aniocha!'

'What do you call men who now live in Aniocha,' asked the herdsman. 'Men? We are shadows.' The herdsman hissed with disgust.

From the woods nearby the dove was heard bewailing again his want of courage. The story goes that he had gone one day to esu (millipede) and asked him to make for him an ogwu that would steel his heart. Esu had obliged. But his ogwu had had no effect and the dove remained his timorous self. Every day he would blame esu for not making him a better ogwu:

'Esu, esu ogwu imelum enwero isu anabu mfu mmadu ume anatum po! po! po! popo-po-po—!'

Some minutes passed and then Okelekwu was seen making his way to the group. He had just jumped a small hedge. As he passed by an ogbu tree in the middle of the ebe one of its leaves dropped on his head.

'Ahai,' murmured Okelekwu. He took up the leaf, tore it and hurled the bits into the dry air.

'Did you see the drummers and the dancers?' Nwora asked as he came up.

'My bones are weary, men of our lands. I didn't know it would be so difficult to get them. "Araba, the big head, I won't beat for him," said one. "I am now a churchman," said another. And the dancers: "We have not danced for some time. Our legs are stiff." Hai! In the days when Araba's hands were full they would have fallen on their knees to be allowed to come and drum for him.'

A year had passed since Araba's death. And none of his sons had come to see about his burial. The omission had remained a blot on the family name. It had also resulted in certain misfortunes, some inexplicable deaths in the kindred. Okelekwu had once gone to the afa and had been told that the spirit of Araba was angry and was saying that because there had been no funeral ceremonies for him, he had not been given his rightful place in spirit-land.

Somebody had better stir, ordered Araba, or he would destroy not only his remiss sons but the whole umunna. The Uwadiegwus had taken fright and had hastily scraped some money in order to make some sort of show. A goat had been sacrificed before Araba's Ikenga and a ceremonial dance had been arranged in the ebe.

'A voice whispered to me that Danda says he would come,' whispered Nwafo.

'Danda? Do they say he is still alive?'

'Very much,' said Okelekwu. 'He has been seen in various lands. They say his name makes noise in Agbenu. And that he has made Umuora his other home. Danda is alive.'

'Akalogholi,' laughed Nwafo. 'It is akalogholis that eat the world.'

The voice of a flute was heard in the distance. A little later, a group of four or five drummers came into the field. They were led by Danda. He hadn't changed much. He was the same tall, almost stooping frame, the same laughing eyes, the same melodious jingle. A new cloak, blue and lined with white, wrapped him. The bronze bells, too, that were attached to it were also new. He wore the anklets of rank and carried an ngwu agelega.

'Kliklikli.'

'Yiii.'

'Kliklikli.'

'Yiii.'

'Rain.'

'God created the world.'

'Son of our fathers,' said Nwokeke, his eyes laughing, 'where did you spring up from?'

'Did they tell you, your father's house is crumbling?' bawled Nwora Otankpa.

'Leave it to me,' said Danda. 'I have come to take possession of my obi and nothing will crumble.'

In the face of such assurance there was nothing more to be said.

'Let's hear the drummers then,' said Nwokeke. 'The day is going home slowly, slowly.'

The drummers found a place, tuned up their instruments and began to play.

Danda stood staring at them with bright-keen eyes, drinking in their tunes. In a moment they began to work on him. The calves of his legs shook, his whole body simmered with excitement. He went mad.

'My father bore me well, my chi created me well.'

Then with his ngwu agelega aloft he danced about and ran the whole length of the ebe shouting.

'Eyo! Eyo!'

The Uwadiegwus at first responded feebly . . . But little by little they became infected with Danda's enthusiasm, and roared back: 'Eyo! Eyo!'

'Ndi beanyi eyo! Eyo!'

'Eyo! Eyo!'

And the drums went on singing:

'Cletum cletum cletum—'

NOTES

The novel is set in Ibo land and there are allusions to Ibo practices which a non-Ibo reader might find difficult to grasp.

To help such a reader a guide seems called for:

The ozo is the highest rank a man may attain to in Ibo land. Among the Ibos status is determined by membership of certain graded societies. Entry to each is bought and the value decides the social standing of the buyer. The ozo society is the highest of these societies, and its members have come to be recognized as the ruling class. In many cases they elect the chief of the village from among their number. They may also serve as the highest court of appeal in the village. An ozo man is recognized by the staff of office which he carries—a bronze spear of intricate design —anklets of rank, and perhaps a cap decorated with parrot's feathers. There are severe penalties against commoners assuming these paraphernalia.

afa: divination

agbada: a Nigerian dress

agbogho mnonwu: a masquerade

agwu: evil spirit or generally, madness

akalogholi: a ne'er-do-well

akpu: cassava food

akwala: a tough fibre from the body of a species of palm

alu: a crime against a taboo (such as incest for instance)

alulani: a crime

Alusi: a god

amosu: an evil bird, a harpy

anini: a farthing

attanis: a roof cover

biko: please

chi: one's personal god

cola: cola nut or generally any refreshment offered to guests

dane-gun: a short locally made gun

dibia: a diviner

ebe: village square

egusi: a type of soup

ekwe: musical instrument

ici: tribal mark

Ijele: a masquerade

Ikenga: one of the *lares*

izaga: a type of masquerade, stands on long stilts

mkpuke: the house where the women live

nama: cowherds

nchi: a large rat

ngwu agelega: ozo staff

nsi: poison charm

obi: the house within the compound where the head of the family lives. It can also mean a man's family heritage.

ocimbo: bleeder

ofo: one of the *lares*, symbolizing a man's belief in his manhood

ogwe: benches made of tree trunks

ogene: musical instrument

ogwu: charm, also medicine. In Ibo both mean almost the same thing

ogwulugwu: a type of music

oibo: 'white' as applied to white man

oja: flute

oji: cola nut offered to guests as customary greetings

ojienu: a masquerade

ojo: the mud bed spread right round the house

onyekulie: a masquerade

ose oji: a paste made of egusi and groundnuts

ozo: an Ibo social rank

palm-fruit light: light made of palm-fruit flowers

umunna: extended family (literally it means children of the same family), kindred.

Fontana African Novels

Elina Obi Egbuna 80p
Modern morality clashes with traditional polygamy in this brilliant satire on life in modern Nigeria.

Emperor of the Sea Obi Egbuna 75p
Five strikingly original stories of Nigeria past and present, by one of her most talented young writers.

The Gab Boys Cameron Duodu 85p
'Mr Duodu lets off shafts at Civil Service corruption, the inadequacies of education, and the absurdities of British life as seen by Africans. The total effect is distinctly entertaining.' *Sunday Times*

Second Class Citizen Buchi Emecheta 85p
'Unquenchable in its spirit . . . piercing observation of Ibo male attitudes and the English treatment of black immigrants.' *West Africa*. 'Brave . . . angry . . . shocking but splendidly undepressing.' *Times Literary Supplement*

The Bride Price Buchi Emecheta 80p
'Humour, affection, irony . . . totally fascinating.' *Times* 'Skilful . . . very real people inhabit her pages.' *West Africa*

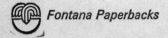 Fontana Paperbacks

Fontana African Novels

The Naked Gods Chukwuemeka Ike 75p
'Brilliant . . . funnily entertaining . . . conflicts in a
university campus, with sex, juju and witchcraft thrown
in for good measure.' *Birmingham Post*

Toads for Supper Chukwuemeka Ike 85p
Scores a bulls-eye for Nigerian writing.' *Guardian.*
'Charmingly funny, touching yet sad . . . executed with
vivacity and deftness.' *Sunday Telegraph*

Sunset at Dawn Chukwuemeka Ike 90p
A satire and a love story as well as a story of battle and
refugee camps, *Sunset at Dawn* is in the definitive novel of
the tragic Biafran war. 'Mr Ike tells a human story with
skill and humour.' *Sunday Times*

The Potter's Wheel Chukwuemeka Ike 75p
'A sympathetic eye for details of family life and local
customs make this a memorable book.' *Daily Telegraph.*
'*The Potter's Wheel* is utterly delicious.' *The Times*

The Interpreters Wole Soyinka 95p
A novel of Nigeria today—from university common-
rooms to society nightclubs to evangelical cults. 'A great
steaming marsh of a book . . . brimful of promise and
life.' *New Statesman*

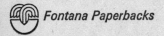 Fontana Paperbacks

Fontana Paperbacks

Fontana is a leading paperback publisher of fiction and non-fiction, with authors ranging from Alistair MacLean, Agatha Christie and Desmond Bagley to Solzhenitsyn and Pasternak, from Gerald Durrell and Joy Adamson to the famous Modern Masters series.

In addition to a wide-ranging collection of internationally popular writers of fiction, Fontana also has an outstanding reputation for history, natural history, military history, psychology, psychiatry, politics, economics, religion and the social sciences.

All Fontana books are available at your bookshop or newsagent; or can be ordered direct. Just fill in the form and list the titles you want.

FONTANA BOOKS, Cash Sales Department, G.P.O. Box 29, Douglas, Isle of Man, British Isles. Please send purchase price, plus 8p per book. Customers outside the U.K. send purchase price, plus 10p per book. Cheque, postal or money order. No currency.

NAME (Block letters)

ADDRESS

While every effort is made to keep prices low, it is sometimes necessary to increase prices on short notice. Fontana Books reserve the right to show new retail prices on covers which may differ from those previously advertised in the text or elsewhere.